THE PREDATOR

On a hill adjacent to the stream they found a game trail. Abundant tracks confirmed deer and elk used it regularly, so Nate let the youth into nearby brush. He didn't think they would have long to wait.

Minutes dragged by. Rabbit Tail sat as motionless as a statue, his ash bow in his left hand, an arrow nocked to the sinew string.

The shadows lengthened. In a little while it would be too dark to shoot reliably. Nate was debating whether to give up the still hunt and rove through the undergrowth when without warning a four-legged apparition materialized on the trail a mere ten yards from their hiding place. He heard Rabbit Tail's sudden intake of breath, and so did the animal.

It was a mountain lion, a large, sleek tawny male, steely muscles rippling as it glided down the trail with its small head lower than its body and its long tail twitching like a serpent. At Rabbit Tail's gasp, the big cat froze, its tail out straight, its nostrils twitching as it tested the air for scent. Suddenly its tail jerked up and the cougar executed a tremendous leap. . . .

The *Wilderness* Series:

#1: KING OF THE MOUNTAIN
#2: LURE OF THE WILD
#3: SAVAGE RENDEZVOUS
#4: BLOOD FURY
#5: TOMAHAWK REVENGE
#6: BLACK POWDER JUSTICE
#7: VENGEANCE TRAIL
#8: DEATH HUNT
#9: MOUNTAIN DEVIL
#10: BLACKFOOT MASSACRE
#11: NORTHWEST PASSAGE
#12: APACHE BLOOD
#13: MOUNTAIN MANHUNT
#14: TENDERFOOT
#15: WINTERKILL
#16: BLOOD TRUCE
#17: TRAPPER'S BLOOD
#18: MOUNTAIN CAT
#19: IRON WARRIOR
#20: WOLF PACK
#21: BLACK POWDER
#22: TRAIL'S END
#23: THE LOST VALLEY
#24: MOUNTAIN MADNESS
#25: FRONTIER MAYHEM
#26: BLOOD FEUD
#27: GOLD RAGE
#28: THE QUEST
#29: MOUNTAIN NIGHTMARE
#30: SAVAGES
#31: BLOOD KIN
#32: THE WESTWARD TIDE

WILDERNESS

Fang & Claw

LEISURE BOOKS NEW YORK CITY

To Judy, Joshua, and Shane

A LEISURE BOOK®

April 2001

Published by

Dorchester Publishing Co., Inc.
276 Fifth Avenue
New York, NY 10001

ISBN 0-8439-4862-0

Visit us on the web at www.dorchesterpub.com.

Fang & Claw

Chapter One

Nate King stepped outside with a heavy Hawken wedged against his broad shoulder. His piercing emerald-green eyes raked the surrounding woodland as his keen ears strained to detect unusual sounds. He saw nothing to explain the strident whinny of his black stallion, which was in a corral on the south side of his cabin.

The big stallion was the next best thing to a watchdog. It nickered whenever anyone approached or when it caught wind of predators.

Sidling along the wall, Nate kept his senses primed. Fringed buckskins clothed his brawny, muscular frame, while his thick thatch of raven hair was crowned by a beaver hat. He moved with the fluid ease and unconscious grace of a man whose sinews had been honed to steely resilience by a life spent on the raw frontier.

A pair of matched flintlocks were tucked under Nate's wide, brown leather belt. Also adorning his narrow waist were a Green River knife and a tomahawk. In effect, he was a walking arsenal. He had to be. Surviving in the wild was no easy task. The wilderness was a harsh mistress. Those who weren't prepared to deal with danger as it arose paid for their folly with their lives.

Nate came to the corner of the cabin. The stallion stood with its head high, ears pricked and nostrils flared, facing east. Again Nate scoured the forest, with the same result.

None of the other horses displayed the least alarm. The mare belonging to Nate's wife was at the water trough slaking its thirst. Several other horses were dozing in the heat of the midday sun. A pack animal was nibbling bits of hay left over from when Nate fed them early that morning.

About to venture into the vegetation, Nate saw the stallion lower its head and relax. Whatever had been out there had evidently gone.

Nate hoped it wasn't another mountain lion. He had striven long and hard to rid his valley of the big cats, just as he had rid his domain of grizzlies. All so his loved ones could move about without fear of being attacked. And while his son, Zach, had recently taken a wife and moved out, Nate still had his wife and daughter to think of.

The stallion pranced over to the rail, begging attention. Nate stroked its neck a bit, gave the terrain a last scrutiny, and retraced his steps, his rifle cradled in the crook of his elbow.

"What was it, Pa?"

Ten-year-old Evelyn was framed in the doorway. As adorable as a kitten, she wore a green dress decorated with white ribbons, fashioned after a picture she had seen in a catalog from St. Louis. Her mother had sewn it using material obtained in trade at Bent's Fort.

"I didn't see hide nor hair of anything," Nate said.

Evelyn's Shoshone heritage showed in her high cheekbones and long, dark tresses, but otherwise she took more after Nate than she did Winona. "Want me to fetch my rifle and we'll go have a look-see?" she asked.

Nate didn't think it was necessary, but it was rare for his daughter to make such an offer, so he said, "Sure. Go ahead. Better safe than sorry."

"I'll be right back." Evelyn scooted off. She was as feisty as a bobcat, but she rarely went hunting or fishing or indulged in activities she deemed "unladylike." Her favorite pastimes were dressing up and playing with her collection of dolls. Which, all things considered, was perfectly normal for a girl her age. But it disappointed Nate sometimes that she didn't have more interest in learning skills more suitable to wilderness life.

Evelyn reappeared trailed by the woman who had claimed Nate's heart nearly two decades ago. To Nate, Winona was every bit as lovely as she had been when he first set eyes on her. A full-blooded Shoshone, she had striking dark eyes and luxurious waist-length hair. A beaded buckskin dress clung to her full, winsome figure, and high moccasins adorned her small feet.

"Is something wrong, husband?"

"I don't think so," Nate said. "We're just going to have a look around."

Evelyn hefted her rifle, a smaller version of Nate's, custom made for her by Sam Hawken himself. It had a short stock and barrel, and took a 36-caliber ball. Which was handy enough for shooting small game, but nowhere near powerful enough to stop a griz or a buffalo. "Ready when you are, Pa!"

Side by side they walked into the trees, Nate smiling inwardly at how earnest and somber she was, with her gun extended and her thumb on the hammer, ready to cock it. "Expecting the Blackfeet to pay us a visit, are you?" he quipped.

"Not really, no." Evelyn avoided a bush that threatened to snag her dress. "It's just that with Zach gone, I have to be of more help to Ma and you."

"You do plenty," Nate said. "You sweep out the cabin

every morning, you help your mother cook and sew, and you have your other chores."

"I don't mean that stuff, Pa. I mean being more like Ma wants me to be."

Puzzled, Nate asked, "And how is that?"

"She thinks I'm too much of a girl."

Drawing up short, Nate put his hand on his daughter's shoulder. "Hold on. Suppose you explain."

Evelyn averted her gaze. "I heard Ma and Zach talking a while back, right before he left to live with Louisa. Ma was saying how she would miss him, how it had been comforting for her to know he was always there to lend you a hand when you needed it."

Nate was still perplexed. "What does that have to do with you?"

"Zach mentioned how I was still here to help. But Ma said it wasn't the same, that I'm not like she was when she was little. I'd rather play with toys than hunt or fish or go riding."

Nate didn't quite know what to say. Winona *was* of the opinion that Evelyn was too prissy for her own good. But then, Winona had been taught to ride almost as soon as she learned to walk. And she had been instructed in how to use weapons in case she was ever called upon to help defend her village. "Comparing yourself to your mother is like comparing acorns and walnuts," he finally said. "You can't judge the worth of one by the other."

"Why not?"

"They're not the same. Neither are you and your ma."

"Maybe so. But I aim to pull my own weight from now on. I'll make Ma proud by being just like she wants me to be."

A comment was on the tip of Nate's tongue, but he didn't utter it. His attention had been drawn to a footprint in a patch of bare, soft soil. Hunkering, he made note of the length, width, and depth, and distinguished a trace of stitching along the outer edge. It told him a great deal.

No two tribes made their moccasins exactly alike. Consequently, seasoned trackers were able to tell which tribe an Indian belonged to by their footwear. In this instance, the print revealed its maker had been a Shoshone warrior—much to Nate's surprise. It was one of his wife's people. Why then was the man skulking around their homestead?

"Is it a Blood or Piegan?" Evelyn asked, referring to allies of the notorious Blackfeet who had given them trouble before.

"No."

"A Ute, then?"

The Utes once claimed the valley. Not long past, however, they had agreed to let the Kings live there unmolested in return for a valuable service Nate did them. "It's a Shoshone," he said, peering off into the brush.

"Someone we know?"

"We'll soon find out." The track was fresh, so fresh that whoever had made it couldn't be far off. Roving about, Nate discovered more and followed them. The warrior had skirted their corral and gone into the trees to the west of the cabin.

Hunkering beside a broad pine, Nate debated whether to go on. He'd rather not expose his daughter to potential peril if he could help it. "We're going back," he whispered. "Stay close and keep your eyes skinned."

"I want to go with you, Pa."

"Nothing doing."

"You're not being fair. You'd let Zach tag along if he were here instead of me."

"Zach is nine years older than you," Nate pointed out.

" 'Fess up. The real reason you won't let me go is because I'm a girl."

There were times, Nate reflected, when Evelyn was remarkably mature for her age. "I won't let you come because I want you with your mother in case there's trouble," he said, which was true as far as it went. Nate

11

took her hand. "No more sass, now." Hunching low, he hurried on around to the front. They were almost to the door when a jay started squawking to the northwest.

"Pa?" Evelyn said.

"I hear it." Nate moved faster, crossing the open space in a quick dash and barreling inside.

Winona was at the counter, skinning a rabbit she had caught in one of the snares she regularly set. When the door crashed open, she jumped, the bloody knife rising to slash and rend. "Husband!"

"We have company," Nate informed her, and bobbed his bearded chin at Evelyn.

Winona caught on right away. "Leave Blue Flower with me," she said, using their daughter's Shoshone name. "We will watch from the window and be ready to help if you need us."

"Bar the door," Nate directed as he slipped back out. Only when he heard the *thunk* of the oak bar sliding into place did he pad to the north. Keenly conscious of how exposed he was, he tried not to dwell on the fact that a carefully aimed shot would easily bring him down. He was glad when he reached the tree line and melted into the jumbled growth.

Moving as stealthily as an Apache, Nate searched for the intruder. The jay had stopped squawking, but now a squirrel in a high spruce was irately chattering a blue streak thirty feet distant. Nate concentrated on the area below the spruce and tensed when a thicket rustled to the passage of a large form.

Hurtling forward, Nate crashed through the thick brush and raced past the spruce, confident he had taken the Shoshone by surprise. But no one was there. Halting in consternation, he peered deep into the thicket, then checked the immediate vicinity.

The squirrel was chittering at *him* now. Nate ignored it and hiked in ever-widening circles, seeking spoor. But the ground was too hard, and the only thing he found was a scuff mark that might or might not have been made by a human heel.

Undeterred, Nate spent the next half an hour diligently scouring the woods adjacent to the cabin. When it proved unproductive, he ventured eastward to a broad lake situated less than a hundred yards from his home.

Ducks and geese milled a stone's throw from shore, a male mallard raising a racket when he appeared.

Nate figured that the intruder might have paid the lake a visit to quench his thirst. He sought sign in the muddy earth at the water's edge, but the only tracks he saw were those of wild animals.

Reluctantly, Nate hiked up the trail linking the lake to the cabin. He had failed, and he did not take failure well. Especially where the safety of his family was concerned. At that very moment, whoever was out there might be watching him and chuckling at his expense.

The door opened before Nate reached it. Winona didn't need to ask how it had gone. She could tell by his expression.

"Maybe the person has gone."

"And maybe elk will learn to fly." Nate gave the woods a last scan, then went in.

Evelyn was over by the fireplace, two of her dolls in hand. One was a brightly dressed maiden, the other a trapper in miniature buckskins, both courtesy of a Shoshone aunt with a wonderful facility for constructing lifelike toys. "Did you catch him, Pa?"

"Not yet."

"You will," Evelyn predicted with all the confidence in the world. "No one ever gets the better of you."

Her faith was charming, typical of a child in a parent, but Nate wasn't about to take anything for granted. Taking a seat at their table, he leaned the Hawken against it. The window afforded him a clear view of the cleared area bordering the front of their home. "At times like this I almost wish Zach hadn't gone off on his own."

13

Winona took a tin cup from their cupboard, filled it with steaming coffee from a batch she had just made, and brought it over. "All fledglings leave the nest eventually," she said in her impeccable English. "I miss him as much as you do. But we have always fought our own fights, husband."

Nate gazed into her lovely eyes. When they first met, he'd never suspected that under her beautiful exterior was a will of steel and courage beyond compare. Over the years she had tangled with bloodthirsty whites and red men alike; she had fought fierce beasts; she had baked in the heat of a desert and nearly froze to death in the frigid ice of winter; yet Winona never complained, never gave in, never allowed life to defeat her. She was the kind of woman any man would be proud to call his mate.

"It is most strange, this warrior," Winona said, sinking down across from him. "He can't be from my village, or he would know you were formally adopted into the tribe. He would know, as my family and friends do, that you are our friend."

Nate grunted in agreement. Her relatives had all paid them a visit at one time or another, most simply to marvel at their log lodge. To the Shoshones, the very idea of a lodge that was rooted to the ground, that couldn't be transported wherever the owner felt inclined to go, was incomprehensible. They had to see it to believe it.

"Maybe he is a Digger," Winona speculated.

The Shoshones, or Snakes, numbered some six thousand. A little more than half dwelled in large villages and subsisted mainly on buffalo. The rest lived deep in the mountains in small communities of two to ten families, surviving on roots, fish, berries, and seeds. "Diggers" the whites called them, poor, timid souls who wore breechclouts and were generally looked down on. While they were regarded as part of the Snake nation, the Diggers were as different from the other Shoshones as night was from day.

Those who, like Winona's people, depended on the buffalo, were a lot like the Plains tribes, like the Sioux, the Cheyenne, the Arapaho. They wore fine buckskins and were armed with bows, lances, and fusees. Rich in horses, they were always on the go, their villages seldom stationary for more than a week to ten days. Other tribes rated their warriors as formidable enemies, high praise by any standard.

Winona's clan belonged to one of the larger, more powerful groups, and their leader, her cousin Touch The Clouds, was a pillar of the Shoshone nation, a warrior of tremendous size and prowess who had become one of Nate's closest friends.

Nate had visited her people countless times. Always, he extended an open invitation to anyone who wanted to return the favor, and scores had taken him up on it. So he couldn't see the intruder being someone who knew him, or even knew *of* him.

Unless the warrior was up to no good.

Suddenly there was a scratching sound at the door.

Nate came up out of his chair as if shot from a canon. Scooping up the Hawken, he flung the door wide, leveling the rifle as he did. But no one was there. Bewildered, he glanced right and left. Then he glanced straight down, and his bewilderment grew.

Winona joined him, her own rifle already cocked. "What is it?"

Nate pointed. "Someone left you a bouquet."

A dozen wildflowers had been deposited at their doorstep, blue and yellow flowers common along the lake. They had been yanked out by the roots, which were packed with dirt, and tied together with a thin strip of buckskin.

Moving into the open, Nate cupped a hand to his mouth and hollered in the Shoshone tongue, "Whoever you are, you need not fear us! We will not harm you! Show yourself!"

The only answer was the sighing of the breeze.

"Could it be Zach?" Winona asked.

Nate had to admit their son was fond of practical jokes, but usually Zach's antics were directed at his sister. It couldn't be Zach for another reason, however. "I know his footprints like I do the back of my hand. The ones I saw were made by someone else. Someone shorter, someone who doesn't weigh as much."

Winona stepped outside. "If you come in peace, prove it!" she shouted. "I give you my word you will be welcome!"

Other than the faint warbling of a sparrow, the woods were silent.

A slender arm looped around Nate's hip and he looked down at the cute button nose of his daughter.

"Maybe it's a trick, Pa," Evelyn said. "Maybe he only wants us to think he's friendly."

"Could be," Nate allowed, even though he doubted it. An enemy wouldn't indulge in such childish antics. "I'm going to have another look around. Stay inside."

Winona opened her mouth as if to object but apparently changed her mind.

"Be careful, Pa," Evelyn said as he padded off.

"My nights would be cold without you," Winona added.

"I'll be back," Nate assured them.

Bathed in the golden glow of the afternoon sun, the valley was tranquil, a Garden of Eden ringed by the stark spires and jagged peaks of the towering Rockies. To the south reared majestic Long's Peak, the highest in the region, its summit mantled by ivory snow even late into the summer. Almost three miles high, it was breathtaking to behold.

Nate warily glided in among the pines. A mix of fir and spruce dominated the valley, interspersed by cottonwoods that thrived along the stream that fed into the lake and around the lake itself. Higher up, on the steep mountain slopes, aspens glittered, their leaves fluttering in the strong breeze.

A variety of wildlife called the valley home. Elk and deer, rabbits, squirrels and other small game were abundant. Fish filled the lake.

It was paradise, a paradise Nate had claimed as his own. He'd fought the Utes and the Blackfoot Confederacy to keep it. He'd battled rogue whites who wanted to force him out. In short, he had done all in his power to preserve it as *his,* and he resented any intrusion.

With renewed determination, Nate searched high and low. He poked into every thicket, checked every gully, behind every knoll. At one time or another he had been over every square foot of that valley, and he knew all the possible hiding places. Yet despite his best efforts, after an hour he still had not found the man who left the flowers.

The longer Nate looked, the angrier he became. No one liked to be made a fool of, and he began to think maybe that was what the intruder was up to. Maybe spooking the horses and leaving the wildflowers were all a bizarre game the man was playing.

Nate held the Hawken ready, leaving nothing to chance. At every noise, no matter how slight, he took a hasty bead, but there was never anyone there. He scolded himself for being jumpy, but he couldn't help it. The tension was grating on his nerves.

After making a complete circuit of the cabin, Nate hiked westward, meandering back and forth in no set pattern, his nose glued to the ground like a bloodhound's. He couldn't say why he had chosen to go west. A hunch, a gut feeling, instinct, whatever it was, he was drawn toward a rocky tract adjoining a high hill. He contemplated climbing to the top, where he would have a clear view of the entire valley.

A dozen yards shy of the hill, Nate registered movement among the boulders. A flash of brown, then it was

17

gone. Reminding himself that it might only be a deer or an elk, Nate cat-footed closer. He saw a vague silhouette deep in the shadows, and the moment he laid eyes on it, the figure angled swiftly upward.

Nate broke into a run, racing to cut off the silhouette. But when he came to where it should have been it wasn't there. Either his eyes had deceived him or the intruder had outwitted him.

Simmering, Nate climbed to the crest, where a panoramic vista unfolded. High stone ramparts on all sides brought to mind a medieval castle. The forest canopy stretched like a verdant carpet, broken at one point by the wide clearing in which the cabin was located. And again by the placid turquoise surface of the lake. Under different circumstances he would be content to stay there a while, entranced by the grandeur and sweep of Creation.

The sharp crack of a twig from the bottom of the hill galvanized Nate into sprinting back down. Off among the boles and boughs, a two-legged shape was visible, running in the direction of the cabin—in the direction of his wife and daughter.

Nate fairly flew, his arms and legs pumping, convinced the intruder had deliberately lured him up the hill so the man could circle around and go after Winona and Evelyn. *Over Nate's dead body!* Without slackening his pace, he vaulted a log and leaped an erosion-worn rut.

The trees began to thin and Nate poured on the speed, gaining gradually on the weaving figure ahead. He was tempted to stop and take aim, but he didn't have a clear shot yet, and any delay in reaching his family might prove costly.

Abruptly, the figure glanced back. Nate glimpsed a weathered, bronzed face that promptly disappeared. One instant the warrior was there, the next he was gone.

Nate dug in his heels and slid to a stop. The intruder had gone to ground. His skin prickling, hunched low, Nate advanced. He had the exact spot pinpointed, but when he got there it was the same story as before.

The mystery man had melted into thin air.

"Damn," Nate swore under his breath. He was tired of being outfoxed and outmaneuvered.

Rustling brought Nate around in a blur. Amid a cluster of trees, a buckskin-clad apparition had materialized. It dodged behind a wide trunk, and Nate gave chase. Heedless of the nicks and cuts and scrapes he received, he plowed through everything and anything in his path.

Once again Nate came to the exact spot where the man had been and, once again, there was no trace of him. Frustrated, Nate sought prints, but the carpet of pine needles underfoot betrayed no clue as to the intruder's whereabouts.

The cabin was only fifty yards away. For all Nate knew, the man might be sneaking toward it at that very second. Out of worry for his wife and Evelyn, he hastened to rejoin them.

Nate was fit to be tied. It was rare for anyone to get the better of him, rarer still for him to be so baffled. Years spent honing his woodlore had endowed him with exceptional tracking ability. Among the mountaineering fraternity he was widely hailed as one of the best trackers alive, which made his failure all the more aggravating.

Pondering how it was possible for the man to have vanished, Nate covered about a dozen yards, then stopped.

An oversight had occurred to him. He'd looked everywhere for his quarry. He'd peered into every bush, inspected every nook. But in his eagerness he had overlooked the obvious, and blundered badly.

Casually turning so as not to forewarn the intruder, Nate retraced his steps. He pretended to be interested in the dense brush to the northeast.

When he was back at the spot where the figure had last been, Nate inspected the ground as if hunting a new sign. The whole time, he swore he could feel eyes boring into him. He hadn't noticed before because his anger had dulled his senses.

Shafts of sunlight filtered through the trees. One of them outlined a squat shadow where there shouldn't be one.

Firming his grip on the Hawken, Nate girded himself. His whole body tingled in expectation of having an arrow or a lance shear into him. "I might as well give up," he said aloud in the Shoshone language to mislead the source of that shadow. Then, pivoting, he spun, elevating the Hawken's muzzle as he did.

Perched on a limb above was his quarry.

Chapter Two

Nate King had confronted countless dangers since settling in the Rockies. He had fought warriors from every hostile tribe there was, as well as some from remote tribes no one had ever heard of. But in all his born days, he had never been outwitted by the likes of the man straddling a thick limb above him.

"Greetings, Grizzly Killer," the stranger said in Shoshone, nervously licking his thin lips like a four-year-old caught with his hand in a cookie jar.

Nate was too flabbergasted to speak. It wasn't that the man knew the Indian name by which he was widely known, since that was to be expected. No, it was the fact that the man on the branch had to be in his seventies or eighties; a slight, frail wisp of a white-haired warrior, well past his prime, yet whose bronzed, wrinkled features were animated by a vitality men half his age would envy.

The old warrior's clothes and style of hair were dis-

David Thompson

tinctly Shoshone, but they had never met, to the best of Nate's recollection.

"I am sorry to have bothered you," the oldster went on. "I came from far off to meet you, but when I saw you, saw how big you were, and remembered the stories they tell of your prowess in battle, I was afraid to impose."

Nate willed his vocal chords to function. "Who are you? What is this all about?"

"I am Teeth Like A Beaver," the warrior declared, and to demonstrate, he smiled broadly. His upper teeth, especially the middle two, were extraordinarily large, long enough and wide enough to do justice to the animal after which he had been named.

"Come down from there," Nate directed, lowering the Hawken. He didn't rate the old-timer much of a threat. The only weapon Teeth Like A Beaver had was a knife in a faded leather sheath.

Wrapping spindly fingers around the limb, the Shoshone began to lower himself. His heel snagged on another branch, throwing him off balance, and he slipped. He would have fallen had Nate not taken a bound and caught him.

"Thank you, Grizzly Killer."

Nate couldn't get over how light the man was, as light as the proverbial feather. "Aren't you a mite old to be clambering around in trees?"

"I have seen ninety-two winters. Or is it ninety-three?" Teeth Like A Beaver scratched his white head. "Sometimes I cannot remember."

"Ninety-two?" Nate repeated, impressed, and set him down. "You are a lot older than I would have guessed."

"May the great Mystery grant you as long a life as I have had," Teeth Like A Beaver said. "I have outlived four wives. I have nine children, twenty-three grandchildren, and too many great-grandchildren to count."

"Is your family nearby?" Nate asked in the belief the oldster couldn't possibly be there alone.

22

"They are at our village many sleeps to the north. If I had told them what I intended to do, they would have tried to stop me. And I could not allow that. So I came alone."

Nate had a lot more questions he wanted to pose but not there. "Why don't you come inside? My wife has coffee on. And we have plenty of jerked venison and pemmican if you're hungry."

"Some food would be nice if it is not an inconvenience," Teeth Like A Beaver said politely. "I have not eaten in two sleeps. Or is it three?"

Nate headed back, the old warrior shuffling at his side. "You were the one who left flowers for my wife?"

"No, I left them for you."

"Me?"

"To show I was a friend. Instead, I offended you somehow. You came into the forest with fire in your eyes, ready to shoot anything that moved. So I hid. But you are as skilled a tracker as everyone says you are. You found me when no one else could have."

Nate saw no need to mention it had been a fluke, more a matter of dumb luck than anything else. "You could have come to our door and knocked."

"Is that how it is done? I did not know. I have never visited a log lodge before and was unsure how to act."

Most whites were unaware Indians adhered to a strict code of lodge etiquette. When the flap was down, it meant the owners did not want to be disturbed. When it was open, visitors were welcome to walk right in. Once inside, male guests were expected to move to the right, women to the left. No one was ever permitted to walk between the fire and another person; it was extremely bad medicine. When invited to a feast, people were required to eat every morsel placed in front of them. And there were other, equally subtle, rules.

"I gather you have not had many dealings with whites," Nate said.

"No, I have not. You are the first white man I have ever spoken to," Teeth Like A Beaver responded. "I did see one once, ten or fifteen winters ago. He was not as big as you, and his beard was not as full. He came to our village asking about beaver. One of our warriors told him where to find them but warned that the Piegans would not like it. The white man went anyway. Later, his bones were found near a beaver pond. His skull had been caved in by a war club. Those Piegans love to kill whites."

As they neared the cabin, the door opened and out stepped Winona, grinning crookedly. "So, husband. This is the fiend who had been terrorizing us?"

"Teeth Like A Beaver, gracious lady," the Shoshone introduced himself. "I apologize for any anxiety I caused you."

"Did you hear me yell earlier?" Winona quizzed. "Did you hear me say you would be welcome if you came in peace?"

"I heard," Teeth Like A Beaver confessed. "But I was scared your husband might shoot me. My mouth would not work, and my legs were like wood."

Evelyn skipped to her mother's side, holding the maiden doll to her bosom. "Howdy, mister," she said in English. Realizing her mistake, she giggled and amended in Shoshone, "My heart is warm to meet a new friend."

"What a pretty child! And such a pretty dress! Never have I seen one the color of grass before."

"This is Blue Flower," Winona informed him.

Teeth Like A Beaver smirked. "Her eyes are green and her dress is green but she is called *Blue* Flower? Interesting." He gazed past them. "Log lodges are much bigger than I imagined. My whole family could fit in there, and my best horse, besides."

"After you," Nate said.

Teeth Like A Beaver hesitated. "Are you sure it is safe? There are no poles to hold the top up. What if it falls?"

"See those big beams?" Nate said. "They brace the

roof. You need not fear. The top will not come crashing down."

"If you say so, Grizzly Killer." But Teeth Like A Beaver was skeptical. Timidly, tentatively, he thrust a foot over the threshold, waited a few moments to verify disaster would not befall him, then slid his other foot across as gingerly as if he were treading on eggshells.

"See? You are still alive."

"So far, yes." Teeth Like A Beaver started to step to the right, but stopped. Gnawing on his lower lip, he started to walk to the left, and stopped again. "What is proper? Where does a guest sit in a white lodge?"

"Anywhere they want."

"Anywhere?" Teeth Like A Beaver surveyed the interior in wonderment, roving from the counter and cupboards to the oak table to the wide, stone fireplace to the frilly curtain that partitioned off Nate and Winona's bed.

"Wherever you will feel comfortable," Nate said. He waited until Winona and Evelyn preceded him, then closed the door and propped the Hawken against the wall. "Our visitor hasn't eaten in a spell. Can you rustle up something for him?" When Winona didn't reply, he turned and saw Evelyn and her staring in amusement at the fireplace.

Teeth Like A Beaver was seated cross-legged *inside* it, on the charred remains of their last fire. He didn't seem to mind the soot-caked sides. Indeed, he was chortling and kept craning his neck to glance up at the ceiling and the broad beams. "This will do quite well," he declared.

Nate went over. "It is where we build our fires."

"Do you need to build one now? I like it here. I do not trust a lodge without poles, and if the top falls, I will be safe."

"Sit there if you want, then," Nate said and moved to his rocking chair. Sinking down, he absently commenced rocking.

Teeth Like A Beaver let out a startled yip. "Truly, this

is a lodge of many marvels! Roofs that stay up without poles! Stone caves for making fires! And now a stool that sways like a tree in the wind!"

Evelyn tittered and roosted beside Nate, remarking in English, "He's funny, Pa. He reminds me of me when I saw hard candy at Bent's Fort for the first time."

Which also reminded Nate. "How about that food, Winona?"

His wife stepped to a row of pegs near the cupboards and took down one of several parfleches. "Pemmican," she said, handing it to the venerable warrior. "Help yourself. In a while I will cook rabbit stew. There is more than enough for all of us, and you are welcome to share."

Teeth Like A Beaver opened the flap, removed a piece, and bit into it. Closing his eyes, he moaned in ecstasy and slowly chewed. "This is some of the best I have ever tasted. My second wife was also good at making it. My third wife always added too much fat, but she was fat herself. She was too fond of eating. I liked to tease her that she never met a buffalo she did not like."

"He has had four wives," Nate mentioned when Winona arched an eyebrow.

"All good women," Teeth Like A Beaver said with his mouth crammed full. "The first was killed. The second was stolen by the Sioux during a raid, by a warrior who must have known a good cook when he saw one." Melancholy seeped into his countenance. "My third wife came down with a fever and never recovered. And the fourth was gored by a buffalo during the last Rose Moon."

Only two months previous, Nate reflected.

The Shoshones divided a year up into twelve moons that roughly corresponded to the traditional twelve-month calender. January was the Snow Moon, fittingly enough. February was the Hunger Moon, the time when food was most scarce. March was the Awakening Moon, when the snow and ice thawed and the land came to life. April had been designated the Grass Moon, May the Planting Moon.

June was the Rose Moon, July the Heat Moon. Due to the frequency of thunderstorms in August, it was the Thunder Moon. September was the Hunting Moon. October, naturally enough, was the Falling Leaf Moon, while November was the Beaver Moon. Coming full circle, December was the Long Night Moon, for obvious reasons.

"You have lived a long, full life," Winona was saying to the old warrior.

"Long, yes. But not as full as I would have liked."

"Four wives is more than enough for most men," Nate jested.

Teeth Like A Beaver smiled rather sadly. "True. But all I ever wanted was one. The first one. The others I married because I was lonely. In time I grew to love each of them, but never as much as I loved the first. She was special." He sighed long and loud. "Our first wives are always our favorites."

"Maybe we should talk about something else," Winona suggested.

"It is all right. My first wife is why I am here."

Nate and Winona swapped glances. "How can that be?" Nate said. "She must have died many winters ago."

"Seventy-two, to be exact," Teeth Like A Beaver said. "Seventy-two winters of missing her every day, of dreaming of her every night."

Winona pulled a chair from the table and sat. "You must have loved her very much," she said softly.

"With all my heart. With all I am. Her name was Bright Morning, and there was never a name more appropriate. She was as beautiful as a waterfall, as kindly as a dove. When I was with her I floated in the air."

"I know the feeling," Nate said, winking at Winona.

"Then perhaps you can forgive me for imposing on you," Teeth Like A Beaver said. "I did not know who else to turn to. My sons refuse to help me. My grandsons say I am being silly, that in my old age my mind is not right. But the young always believe they know more than those who taught them all they know."

"What is it they will not help you do?" Nate prodded when the old warrior fell quiet.

"Die."

Winona straightened. "You want to kill yourself?"

"No. You misunderstand. I do not want to die, but I have no choice. My time has come. There is something inside me, something that eats at me and makes me weak and dizzy. Our healer tried to cure me, but his herbs did not work. Soon I will be no more. Soon I will go to be with my beloved Bright Morning."

Nate still didn't get it. "Why is that silly?"

"It is not the dying that my family thinks is silly, it is where I want to die. I want to be buried beside Bright Morning."

Now Nate thought he understood. Shoshones didn't bury their dead in the white manner. Bodies were washed and wrapped in clean blankets, then concealed in crevasses or other crannies where scavengers couldn't get at them. The Shoshones never adopted the custom other tribes had of hoisting their dead up in trees or on specially made platforms. "Your sons and grandsons will not honor your request?"

"They say I should be content to die among my people. They say where I want to go is too far. They say it is too dangerous."

"Where is this place?"

"To answer that, I must tell you a story," Teeth Like A Beaver responded. "The story of how I lost Bright Morning. The story of the worst day of my life. Do you mind?"

"We will be glad to hear it," Winona said.

The white-haired warrior took another bite of pemmican before beginning. "As I told you, it was seventy-two winters ago. Long before the coming of the whites. Back when great men like Whoshakik and Inkatushepo led our people, and the Blackfeet quaked in fear when we went on the warpath."

Nate recollected hearing about Whoshakik; the Shoshones loved to sit around lodge fires late at night and swap tales of the old days.

"Bright Morning had been my wife for two winters. We were as happy as two people could be, but I was not content. I wanted to rise in standing in the tribe. I wanted to prove myself, to show I was worthy of becoming a leader."

"By counting coup?" Nate said. Invariably, the warrior who counted the most was widely esteemed and ranked high in tribal councils.

"Counting enough to matter takes time, time I did not want to waste. I was young. I was headstrong and impatient. I wanted to be great, but I wanted it then and there. So I came up with what I thought was a better way. A faster way." The melancholy returned. "Bear Canyon."

"I have never heard of it," Nate admitted.

"I have," Winona interjected. "It is an old legend. A canyon my people shunned because it was home to the grandfather and grandmother of all bears. Bears twice as large as the biggest grizzly. Bears like no others ever seen."

Nate's interest perked. "Is there any truth to the tale?"

It was Teeth Like A Beaver who answered. "Bear Canyon is real. I have been there. I saw one of the beasts with my own eyes. A bear almost as big as your log lodge. It could rip a man or woman in half with one swipe of its paws."

An exaggeration, if ever Nate heard one. But his curiosity climbed. "Tell us your story."

Teeth Like A Beaver shifted, making himself comfortable. "When I let Bright Morning know my plan, she was upset. She tried to persuade me not to go. She said I was in too much of a rush to become great. And I, in my stupidity, would not listen. I thought I knew better than

29

she did. So I went to see Yellow Hand, the oldest warrior in our tribe. At the time, he was older than I am now, so old he could not stand without a cane. So old, all his teeth had fallen out."

"He knew where Bear Canyon was?"

"Yellow Hand had been there once when he was sixteen winters old. He had gone with his father and six other warriors to see for themselves if the stories were true." Teeth Like A Beaver gazed off across the room as if gazing back through the mists of time. "Yellow Hand was the only one who came back."

"Did he say what happened?"

"His father's party camped by a stream that flows through the canyon. That first night, the grandfather of all bears attacked them. Yellow Hand had gone into the trees to gather firewood and was walking back. He witnessed the whole thing. He saw his father torn apart and eaten."

"How did he describe the bear?"

"It was gigantic, just as the legends claim. When it walked, the ground thundered. When it breathed, it gave off steam. Arrows and bullets had no effect."

Evelyn was listening in rapt fascination. "Did you still want to go there after he told you all that?"

"Yes, little one," Teeth Like A Beaver said. "I thought it could not possibly be true. More than ever, I wanted to slay one of the great bears to prove my own greatness."

"You took your wife along?" This from Winona in a tone of reproach.

"She refused to be left behind. I told her to stay. One morning I rode off alone, but she followed. She shadowed me for over a day, until we were so far from the village, she was confident I would not turn around and take her back. To my sorrow, I did not."

"She must have loved you very much," Winona said.

The old Shoshone's eyes misted over and he swallowed a few times before continuing. "She loved me as dearly as I loved her. Later, she proved how much when she—"

Fang and Claw

He stopped. "I am getting ahead of myself. We rode for eight sleeps, and on the ninth day we came to the passage into Bear Canyon."

"Was it hard to find?" Nate figured it had to be. For years white trappers had ranged over every square foot of the mountains in pursuit of beaver, and none ever reported encountering bears remotely similar to those in the Shoshone legend.

"Not if a man knows where to look. Had it not been for Yellow Hand, I would never have found it." Teeth Like A Beaver paused. "Coyote, in his wisdom, tried to spare fools like me by hiding the canyon where none would suspect."

Nate idly stroked his mustache. According to Shoshone belief, Coyote was the father of their people. In ancient times, Coyote had married a cannibal, a girl who like to kill and eat everyone who paid her a visit, and the fruits of their union were the first Shoshones.

The old warrior had gone on. "I tried to convince Bright Morning to wait for me outside Bear Canyon, but she refused. We rode on in, and although I searched long and hard for bear signs that day, we saw none. To be safe, I made camp on a rocky shelf midway up a steep slope. Nothing could get at us without making noise, which would give us time to run to safety. Or so I thought."

"What was the canyon like?" Nate wanted to know.

"A vile place. All the evil in the world dwells there. It chills the spirit and makes brave hearts weak. In my ignorance, I pretended I was not afraid. I refused to do what I should have done—leave."

Evelyn bent forward, her elbows on her knees. "Did you see the giant bears?"

"I will get to that, pretty one." Teeth Like A Beaver's shoulders slumped and his voice lowered. "For three sleeps all went well. I searched and searched but found no sign of them. I had begun to think maybe Yellow Hand had not told the truth, or else the bears had died off. But

31

the next day, when I led our horses down to the stream to drink, I saw tracks. Bears prints so big, I could sit in them. With claws as long as my knife."

"Surely you decided to leave then?" Winona interrupted. "For Bright Morning's sake, if nothing else."

"Would that I had," Teeth Like A Beaver said forlornly. "But when I saw the tracks, all I could think of was how famous I would be if I brought the bear's hide to my people. My name would be on every tongue, and I would be hailed as the bravest warrior alive."

"Pride goeth before a fall," Nate quoted in English.

"What was that?" the warrior said.

"Nothing," Nate replied in Shoshone. "Sorry. Go on. Please."

Teeth Like A Beaver was a long time doing so. "I thought I was clever. I set a trap by rigging boulders to topple down the slope when I wanted them to. I shot a buck, gutted it, and left it lying at the bottom as bait. Then I climbed to our shelf and we waited."

"Weren't you afraid?" Evelyn wondered.

"Very much so. But I did not let on that I was. I hugged Bright Morning and assured her I had everything under control. I promised her all would be well. And she believed me. She looked up at me with her beautiful eyes and she said, 'I trust you.'" The warrior coughed and said again, so quietly they could barely hear him, "'I trust you.'"

No one else spoke, and after a bit Teeth Like A Beaver resumed his account. "All that day we waited and watched, but the bear did not appear. The sun started to set, and across the canyon I saw something coming through the forest. Something huge. Something higher than I would be if I were standing on my horse. A creature that snapped trees like kindling. It was the grandfather of all bears."

"How do you know it wasn't the grandmother?" Evelyn said.

A wan grin spread across the old Shoshone's face. "Maybe it was, child. The shadows in the canyon were long and deep, and when it came to the stream, I could not see it clearly. It drank, then raised its enormous head and sniffed the air. The scent of blood drew it to the buck, and it feasted." Teeth Like A Beaver shuddered. "We could hear the crunch of bones, the rending of hide."

"How awful," Winona commented.

"I crawled to the boulders I had rigged. There were four, each as big as I was. But the bear devoured the buck so fast, it was almost done eating when I reached the first one. I kicked the limb that held it in place and saw it tumble, saw it smash the bear in the head. But the brute did not go down. Instead, the bear roared, a roar heard from one end of the earth to the other. And it charged." Tears trickled down the warrior's wizened cheeks. "I sent the other boulders crashing down, but they bounced of it like pebbles. Next I remember the bear rearing above me. I remember hearing Bright Morning scream my name and seeing her rush to help. Then there was a blow to my head, and all that night I was unconscious. When I awoke the bear was gone. Why it spared me, I will never know. But I wish it had not."

"What about Bright Morning?" Winona breathlessly inquired.

"Bits and pieces of her were all over the shelf. I also found her gnawed thigh bone by the stream. I buried all I could collect on the shelf."

"How terrible," Evelyn said. "I feel so sorry for you."

Nate had a terrible feeling, too, an insight into why the old warrior had traveled so far to see him. He hoped he was wrong, but he had to find out. "What is it you want of me?"

Teeth Like A Beaver slid from the fireplace and slowly unfurled. With tears in his eyes, he clasped Nate's hand and said in earnest appeal, "I came to ask you, Grizzly Killer—no, to *plead* with you—to take me to Bear Canyon and put me to rest beside Bright Morning."

Chapter Three

"Surely you are not thinking of doing it, are you?"

It was an hour after supper. Nate had stepped outside to think and was leaning with his back against the corral when Winona joined him and posed her question. He was reluctant to admit the truth, and his hesitation confirmed her hunch.

"Was it something in the stew?" Winona said, but neither of them laughed. "I credited you with more common sense."

"He wants to pass into eternity next to the woman he loved most in this world," Nate responded. "What's wrong with that?"

"Everything, if it gets you killed." Normally so composed, Winona's exasperation showed in the twitch of her jaw and her rigid posture. "You chance throwing your life away to help someone you hardly know."

"He's a fellow Shoshone. I owe it to him to do what I can."

Winona's warm fingers closed on Nate's hand. "I admire the sentiment, but it is misguided. Even his own family will not help him. Neither should you."

"What if it had been you who died in that canyon? I'd want to do the same thing Teeth Like A Beaver is doing."

Winona pressed against him and affectionately pecked his cheek. "Always putting yourself in the moccasins of others, is that it? But in this instance you should not let your heart rule your mind. If you were thinking clearly you would realize too much is stacked against you."

"Such as?"

"Such as there is no guarantee he can find Bear Canyon. It has been over seventy years and his memory, by his own admission, is not what it once was. But let us suppose he does. I doubt he will drop dead the minute you find the shelf where he buried Bright Morning. And the longer you stay there, the greater the risk of running into one of those bears."

"Maybe. Maybe not. Grizzlies only live about thirty years at the most. The one he saw and any others around at the time are long since dead by now."

"If they *were* grizzlies."

"What else could they be?" Nate said. "Black bears?" The notion was ridiculous. Black bears were much smaller than grizzlies and usually fled at the mere sight of a human being.

"Maybe they are the bears of old," Winona stated.

"You've lost me."

"My people have many legends besides Bear Canyon. Long ago, when the first Shoshones explored this new land, it was overrun by fierce animals. Monsters, you would call them. Elephants like those mentioned in that book you have, only these were hairy, with long, curved tusks. Boars the size of horses. Horses the size of dogs. And the bears of old, bigger than buffalo and many times more savage than grizzlies."

Nate had learned not to mock Shoshone legends, but

35

there were limits to how much he would accept without evidence. "How have these old bears, as you call them, survived so long? Why didn't they die off with the rest of the creatures of long ago?"

Winona shrugged. "Who can say? There are many places in the mountains where no one ever goes, white man or red. Dark places. Secret places. Places better left undisturbed. Bear Canyon is one of them." She studied him a moment. "There's more to this, isn't there?"

"How do you mean?"

"Don't play innocent. A wife always knows when her husband is holding something back." Winona's brow furrowed. "It's the bears, isn't it? You want to see for yourself if they are real."

Nate was going to tell her not to be silly, but the words died in his throat. Never once, in all the years of their marriage, had he ever lied to her. He wouldn't do so now. "To be honest, yes, I would."

"Do you have a death wish?"

"Be serious."

"Then why on earth would you want to do such a thing?"

"How can I explain?" Nate turned and rested his arms on the top rail, his chin on his wrist. "I've had more than my share of scrapes with bruins, as you well know. Through no hankering on my part, I've killed more silvertips than any man alive—"

"All the more reason," Winona broke in, "for you to recognize how foolish your wish is. You barely survived some of those scrapes. Why tempt fate by deliberately courting another?"

"Do you remember, years ago, when I had a run-in with a giant grizzly that everyone claimed was the biggest in the Rockies?"

"I remember you were lucky to escape with your life."

"Well, now I've learned there might be some even bigger. Call it stupid. Call me a jackass. But I have an urge to prove whether the legend is true or not. It's that simple."

"Is it?" Winona pursed her lovely lips. "Or is it that you think you have something to prove to yourself?"

"For instance?"

"You are the famous Grizzly Killer. You have bested every bear you ever went up against. Could it be that you want to pit yourself against the grandfather of all bears to prove to yourself that you can best him, as well? That you are truly worthy of your name?"

"Give me more credit than that, will you?"

"I would like to. But this worries me. It is not like you to trifle with danger. You have always had a good head on your shoulders." Winona mustered a grin. "A handsome head, I might add." She traced the edge of his right ear with her finger. "It would distress me considerably were you to lose it."

Chuckling, Nate pulled her close and kissed her full on the lips. "Has anyone ever mentioned that you're the most wonderful woman who ever lived?"

"Flatterer." Giggling, Winona kissed him, then said severely, "But don't change the subject, husband. I need to know what you plan to do."

"I honestly don't know. I told Teeth Like A Beaver I would think it over and give him my answer in the morning." Nate gazed at the myriad of sparkling stars that filled the firmament. "Is he still sleeping?"

"Yes, curled up in the fireplace. His buckskins will be covered with soot when he wakes up. I'll offer to clean them for him."

"He'll be crushed if I tell him no."

"So? Rather that, than have *you* be crushed under the paws of the grandfather of all bears." Winona gripped him by the shoulders. "I love you. I do *not* want to lose you." When he didn't say anything, she shook him as if she were angry, but the emotion her eyes radiated belied any such motive. "You are the most decent, noble man I know. You are pure of heart, and as devoted a father and husband as any woman could ever want. You are my life, Nathaniel King, and if you die, I die."

Tremendously moved, Nate embraced her. For long minutes they stood locked together, her cheek on his chest.

"Are you two smooching again?"

Nate hadn't heard their daughter walk up. Glancing down, he smiled and said, "What if we were?"

"It's yucky. If any boy ever tries to kiss me, I'll bust him right in the mouth." Evelyn had her doll under her arm and was nibbling on a piece of jerked venison. "I came out to see what was keeping Ma so long. I should have known."

Winona crooked a finger under Evelyn's chin. "Sometimes, little one, you are too precocious." Grinning, she headed indoors. "I'll clean the supper dishes. You can keep your father company."

Evelyn gazed at Nate. "What's precocious mean, Pa?"

"I think it means you're cute, but I'm not totally sure."

"How is it Ma know so many words that you don't?"

"I wouldn't go that far," Nate said, miffed. "She spends a lot of time reading the dictionary, is all."

Evelyn peered through a gap in the rails at the dozing horses. "So, when do we leave for Bear Canyon?"

"We?"

"You're going to go. Ma said she can feel it in her bones. She also said where you go, she goes, and where she goes, I go. So when do we leave?"

"I haven't even decided whether I will take him yet."

"It's the right thing to do."

"You think?"

"Haven't you always taught me to help others when they need it? And doesn't it say in the Bible that we're supposed to do unto people—" Evelyn paused, uncertain. "How does it go again?"

"Do unto others as you would have them do unto you."

"That's the one. You've been reading to me from the Good Book since I was old enough to recollect. I always thought you did it because you want me to live as it says to live. But now you're saying we shouldn't?"

Kids could ask the darnedest questions, Nate mused. "There are a lot of folks who don't give a hoot about Scripture. And I've got to admit, I haven't always lived by the Golden Rule. But, yes, we should always try our best. A lot of times we'll fall short. A lot of times we do things without really thinking about whether it's right or wrong. The important thing is that we try."

"So how can you even think of not helping Teeth Like A Beaver?"

Nate put a hand on her hair and tenderly ruffled it. "Out of the mouth of babes," he said, more to himself than to her.

"What are you talking about? I'm no baby. I'm pretty near half grown."

Picking Evelyn up, Nate strolled toward the cabin. "In some ways, daughter-of-mine, you're more grown up than some adults I've met." He squared his shoulders. "Let's go in and break the bad news to your mother."

"Bad? But you're doing good."

"Tell that to her."

As was his habit, Nate awoke at first light. He rolled out of bed without disturbing Winona, who had slept with her back turned to him. A sure sign she was upset, although she hadn't let on that she was when he informed her of his decision.

Donning his buckskins, Nate tucked a pair of flintlocks under his belt and walked outside, quietly closing the door behind him so as not to awaken the others.

The new day was dawning crisp and clear. Pillowy clouds sailed overhead in a lake-blue sky. A breeze rustled the tops of the trees, and down at the lake the ducks and geese were in full chorus, greeting the morning in their typical raucous manner.

Stretching, Nate rubbed his chin. He had a lot to do before he could leave; shoe the horses, prepare the provisions, check his possibles bag. He figured on traveling light, on only taking the stallion and the old Shoshone's mount. Pack animals would only slow them down and weren't needed anyway since the two of them could live off the land with no problem.

Yawning, he shifted, and received a surprise.

Over by the trail that led to the lake stood Teeth Like A Beaver. His arms were upraised, his face to the sun, his eyes closed. He was softly chanting, so softly that Nate only caught a few of the words, but they were enough to spur him into going over. Out of courtesy, Nate waited for the warrior to finish.

Teeth Like A Beaver cracked an eyelid. "You have something to say?" he asked, and continued chanting.

"What are you doing?"

"Practicing my death chant. What does it sound like?"

"That is what I thought. Are you in so great a hurry to die?"

The Shoshone lowered his arms. "There are four great moments in a man's life, my new friend. When he is born. When he sleeps with a woman for the first time. When he counts his first coup. And when he dies. We have no control over our birth, so we enter this world with no dignity at all, kicking and bawling. I do not propose to go out of this world the same way. I will sing my song, lie down, and await my end with as much dignity as I can."

"Dignity is important to you, is it?"

"As it should be to everyone. If a person has not learned to respect himself, how can he learn to respect others?" The wind fanned Teeth Like A Beaver's white hair. "When I counted my first coup, I did so in as dignified a manner as I could. I did not shoot my foe from ambush.

I faced him and fought him in fair combat. And when he fell, I did not yell and laugh as some do. I gave thanks, then took his scalp."

"What about the other great moment?" Nate asked for humor's sake. "How dignified were you when you slept with a woman for the first time?"

Teeth Like A Beaver chortled. "That was hopeless. I had butterflies in my stomach. My mouth was dry and I broke out in sweat. When I kissed her, in my enthusiasm I split her lip. But Bright Morning never held it against me." He glowed at the remembrance. "I cannot wait to see her again."

"Do you believe there is life after death?" Nate knew most Shoshones did, which had astonished him immensely him when he initially met them. In the States, Indians were branded as "heathens" doomed to perdition, with no concept of the spirit or the soul, but that wasn't the case.

Shoshone belief centered around Coyote. After they died, their spirits would leave their bodies and be met by another spirit that would escort them to the land of Coyote, where they would live happily forever.

The Shoshones also believed there was one higher than Coyote. Apo, they called him. The whites translated it as Great Spirit, but a more fitting name was Great Medicine or Great Mystery.

Teeth Like A Beaver had more to say. "Show me a man who does not believe in an afterlife and I will show you a man who does not use his brain. My friend, Buffalo Meat Under The Shoulder, visited it once, and when he came back he told me all about it."

"When he what?"

"It was forty winters ago or more. He had a vision in which Apo informed him he would die. So for three days and three nights Buffalo Meat Under The Shoulder lay in his lodge, waiting for it to happen. On the fourth day his soul came out of his body. He went to another world and

David Thompson

followed a trail that brought him to Father, to Coyote. Father had a wire that made a lot of noise. When Father tapped it three times, the whole world opened up, and Buffalo Meat Under The Shoulder could see everything. But then Father looked at him and said, 'You are not very ill.' At that, Apo told my friend he would be restored to life, and the next moment he was."

"Was there anything else he remembered?"

"There was a lot more. But Buffalo Meat Under The Shoulder did not understand much of what he saw. He did say that Father was very handsome." Teeth Like A Beaver smiled. "Bright Morning is in that land, waiting for me."

"Did your friend see any whites there?" Nate asked, knowing full well the answer he would get.

"You joke with me. As an adopted Shoshone, Grizzly Killer, you must know that whites go to a different place when they die. A lower place, it is said. But you need not worry. You will travel to Coyote's land like we do."

To Nate it didn't much matter whether it was Heaven or Coyote's Land so long as he was reunited with Winona. "You and I are much alike in some regards," he remarked.

Teeth Like A Beaver frowned. "Would that we were. Would that I were a mighty slayer of bears like you. I might have killed the grandfather of all bears that day in Bear Canyon. Bright Morning would not have died."

"Stop blaming yourself," Nate said, but the old Shoshone seemed not to hear him.

"That is why I came to you for help. People say you are a friend to all. They say you are a man without fear. That you slay bears as others swat insects." Teeth Like A Beaver gripped Nate's arm. "You are the one person who can help me. If you had refused, I planned to tie big rocks to my ankles, hop into the lake, and drown myself."

"Where is the dignity in that?"

"There is none," Teeth Like a Beaver conceded. "But I will die soon, anyway. And if I can not be lain to rest

42

with Bright Morning, what use is there for me to go on? You were my last hope. I thank Coyote you did not turn me down." He looked toward the cabin. "Someone else is up."

Smoke wafted from the chimney in lazy curls. "Winona is fixing breakfast. Are you hungry?"

"I could eat a horse. Your wife is an outstanding cook. Were I you, I would be as heavy as a buffalo." Teeth Like A Beaver inhaled deeply, his small chest expanding. "How strange that when I am on the verge of death, I find so much joy in life."

Nate checked on the horses prior to going in. The night before, he had gone with Teeth Like A Beaver into the pines to where the warrior had left his mount, a sorrel as advanced in years as its owner.

Hay was stored in a shed at the rear of the corral. The same shed that housed a small forge Nate used on occasion to make new horseshoes and do metalwork. Taking the pitchfork, he tossed hay to the waiting horses. They had the daily routine down pat and always milled at the rail as soon as the sun rose.

Teeth Like A Beaver scanned the valley. "You have chosen your home wisely, Grizzly Killer. A man could have a good life here."

"We get by," Nate said, spearing the pitchfork into the mound again. "Our lodge was built by my uncle, who was killed by the Utes. Later I added onto it."

"The Utes used to be bad people. They were always on the war path against us. But in recent winters they have grown friendly. Their new chief, Two Owls, is a man of wisdom and peace."

"I know. He is a friend of mine," Nate said. It was in large measure because of their friendship that the Ute leader had made peace overtures to the whites and the Snakes.

For the third time Nate hoisted hay over the rails. As he did, he happened to gaze toward the mountains to the

43

north, toward a sawtooth ridge barren of trees, and involuntarily tensed. Riders were coming over it.

"What caught your eye?" Teeth Like A Beaver said, gazing in the same direction. "Ah. Friends of yours?"

"There's no telling." Nate's son lived in a valley to the northwest but wasn't due to visit for another couple of weeks. An old friend by the name of Shakespeare McNair had a cabin miles to the north, but again, McNair and his Flathead wife were not expected anytime soon. Besides which, McNair rode a white horse, and it was plain to Nate that none of the animals on the ridge were white.

Jamming the pitchfork into the mound, Nate left it there and walked on around the corral. He estimated it would take the better part of an hour for the riders—four of them—to reach his homestead. By then he would have a suitable reception arranged.

Teeth Like A Beaver bustled to keep up. "You do not like visitors much, do you, Grizzly Killer?"

"What makes you say that?"

"You are wearing the same face you did yesterday when you hunted for me. Do you have many friends? Or have you scared most of them off?"

"I have my family to consider," Nate said. "I can't welcome strangers with open arms. Too many have tried to rub us out." Halting, he watched the riders wind lower down the mountain. "My outlook is be friendly but keep my guns oiled and loaded."

Teeth Like A Beaver laughed. "I like that. When I was younger, my way was to offer the pipe of peace but keep a knife up my sleeve."

Now it was Nate who laughed. "Do you have a knife up your sleeve now?"

"Up both sleeves."

Nate patted the warrior's forearms, and sure enough, he felt hard, slender objects under the buckskin. Recalling how the oldster had eluded him the day before, he said by way of a compliment, "You sure are tricky."

"Thank you. Coyote, our Father, is also known as the Trickster, remember."

Winona came out, as radiant as the morning sun, a wooden spoon caked with flour in her hand. "Breakfast will be ready soon, husband," she said in English. "Flap-jacks and syrup, just as you like."

"Better hold off for a while," Nate said, bobbing his chin at the ridge.

Shielding her eyes with her free hand, Winona took stock of the newcomers. "They are Indians, not whites. A war party, you think?"

"Riding right up to us in broad daylight?" Nate doubted it, but it could be a ruse. "We'll know soon enough, I reckon."

Forty-five minutes later the riders came into sight among the trees, riding in single file. All were men. Two were armed with bows slung across their backs. The other two carried lances tipped with feathers.

Nate waited in the open, his Hawken cradled in his arm, his right hand on a pistol at his waist. Over at the window was Winona, her own rifle plainly visible. Evelyn and Teeth Like A Beaver had been instructed to stay inside and keep low.

The lead warrior spotted Nate and drew rein. A stocky man in his mid to late forties, he twisted and said something to his companions, then jabbed his heels against his bay. He did not unsling his bow or make any other threatening moves.

The quartet were almost to the clearing when Nate determined they were Shoshones. Oddly, each was younger than the man in front. The second rider, a bean pole wearing beaded leggings, looked to be in his thirties. The warrior behind him was in his twenties, and the last rider couldn't be more than fifteen or sixteen. When they reached the edge of the clearing they reined up again and glanced at the cabin with a degree of apprehension. The youngest nervously fidgeted, acting almost scared. None made any attempt to employ a weapon.

Nate waited for them to demonstrate their intentions.

The oldest man smiled. His hands moved in fluid sign language, or hand talk as some called it, the well-nigh universal language relied on by most of the Plains and many of the mountain tribes. "We come peace."

"I can tell," Nate said in Shoshone.

"You speak our tongue," the man responded in kind. "Perhaps we have finally found the one we seek. I am Only Hunts Elk." He jabbed his thumb at the bean pole with the fancy leggings. "This is Man Without A Wife, my brother." His thumb jabbed at the next oldest. "That is Humpy, another brother. And last is Rabbit Tail, my son."

Nate allowed himself to relax. "I am Grizzly Killer."

The four Shoshones glanced at one another in delight, and Only Hunts Elk said: "We are pleased to meet you. We have traveled far, ridden long and hard. Six sleeps ago we stopped at the village of Touch The Clouds, and he told us where we could find your log lodge."

"Climb down." Nate beckoned. "You are welcome to stay and share my food."

"We are grateful," Only Hunts Elk said. "But before we do, there is something we must know."

Man Without A Wife gestured impatiently. "Ask him and be done with it."

Before Only Hunts Elk could respond, a low groan emanated from behind Nate, a groan of abject misery. Pivoting, Nate saw Teeth Like A Beaver at the cabin door, clutching his stomach as if he were ill. "Are you sick?"

"Worse!" the old warrior declared. "What I feared has come to pass! Save me, Grizzly Killer! Drive them off before it is too late!"

Chapter Four

If Nate King didn't know better, he would swear Teeth Like A Beaver was about to be set upon by a horde of bloodthirsty Blackfeet. "Save you from what?" he asked, although he suspected the truth.

"I can answer that," Only Hunts Elk said, kneeing his mount forward. The others took that as their cue to do likewise. "He thinks we are here to take him back."

"Curs! Worms! Lice!" Teeth Like A Beaver railed. "Quit plaguing me! Leave an old man in peace!"

The four men reined up near Nate, and Only Hunts Elk let out with the sigh to end all sighs. "Why do you persist in embarrassing us like this? Why must you always behave as if you are five years old?"

Teeth Like A Beaver flushed with indignation. "Did you hear him, Grizzly Killer? The seed of my loins showing such disrespect for his own father! Tell them to leave. And if they refuse, shoot one of them in the leg to persuade them."

Rabbit Tail glanced at Nate as if afraid Nate would do as the old man wanted. "If you want them shot," Nate said, "you will have to shoot them yourself."

"Give me your gun then!" Teeth Like A Beaver snatched at the Hawken, but Nate pulled it away. "We must drive them off. They are meddlers, one and all. I am ashamed to claim them as mine."

Man Without A Wife scowled. "*You* are ashamed? How do you think we feel? You are a doddering, feeble fool, father, who should be tied to a stake so he cannot wander off and do harm to himself."

"Fool, am I?" Shaking his fists, Teeth Like A Beaver made as if to throw himself at his son, but Nate grasped his arm. "If I were ten years younger, I would pull you down from there."

"I would like to see you try."

Livid, Teeth Like A Beaver tried to break loose from Nate. "Let me go! He has always been an ungrateful whelp. He has this coming."

"*ENOUGH!*" Only Hunts Elk commanded with an air of finality. "Father, you will act your age. Man Without A Wife, you will apologize to him."

"I would rather have my hair lifted by the Crows," the bean pole grumbled.

Teeth Like A Beaver, shaking with suppressed wrath, stopped trying to pull free. "I should have died with Bright Morning. I never should have lived to see the day when my own sons would treat me like a maggot."

Only Hunts Elk faced Nate. "I am sorry, Grizzly Killer. These two have been at each other's throats since Man Without A Wife was in a cradleboard. The people of our village are as tired of it as I am."

Nate wasn't surprised. Among the Shoshones, public displays of anger were virtually unheard of. From an early age Shoshone children were taught to control their temper. Parents impressed on them that to ruin the harmony of the village was a grave breach of tribal etiquette. Unlike whites, who passed hundreds of laws each year in a futile bid to force people to live civilly, the Shoshones relied more on teaching by example and the pressure brought to bear by family and friends. Lapses were rare.

Clearing his throat, Nate said, "All of you are my guests, and from here on, you will act as guests should. No more yelling. No more name-calling. Agreed?" He looked at Teeth Like A Beaver and Man Without A Wife. When neither replied, he said again, much more sternly, "Do you agree?"

"I will honor your request," Man Without A Wife said none too happily.

Teeth Like A Beaver, though, stamped his foot like a petulant child. "I would rather shoot him in the leg."

"Your word," Nate said. "Or they can take you home right this moment."

Spite drained from the old warrior like water from a sieve. "You would do that to me, Grizzly Killer?" he asked in shock. "Knowing how much it means to me to be buried beside Bright Morning?"

"Your word."

"You have it. I will behave myself if they do," Teeth Like A Beaver said begrudgingly.

The four men climbed down. At Nate's suggestion, they led their weary animals to the corral, and while they were occupied, he went inside to explain the situation to Winona.

"What will you do if they insist on taking him back?" she inquired.

"I don't rightly know," Nate confessed. He had no business butting into a family squabble. On the other hand, he had promised to take Teeth Like A Beaver to Bear Canyon, and he was a man of his word.

Evelyn was in the rocking chair, clasping one of her ever-present dolls. Today she had on a blue dress and her hair was decorated with a pair of matching blue ribbons. "Morning, Pa."

"Morning, princess." Nate went over and kissed her on the forehead. "It appears we have more visitors."

"I heard. Folks in St. Louis probably heard, too."

The four warriors appeared at the doorway. Teeth Like A Beaver had already entered and was sulking by the fireplace, unable to climb in it because Winona had a fire going.

Teeth Like A Beaver's sons and grandson were as uneasy about the cabin as the old man had been. Only Hunts Elk entered first, slowly, edgily, as he would were he entering a grizzly's den. Humpy followed, gaping at the furniture. He had full cheeks, like a chipmunk's, and wore half a dozen beaded necklaces. Man Without A Wife glared at their father, who glared right back. Last, and most skittish of all, was Rabbit Tail. Fascinated by the floorboards, he kept tapping his foot as if afraid they would buckle under his weight.

Nate grabbed hold of the table and dragged it to one side, clearing a wide space. "Sit if you would like," he said, and did so himself, sinking straight down. The Shoshones did the same, all except for Teeth Like A Beaver, who stayed aloof.

As the oldest son, Only Hunts Elk had the right to speak on behalf of the whole group. He started by stating, "We are honored to be invited into your wooden lodge, Grizzly Killer. We have heard much about you, about your prowess in battle and your ability as a hunter. If you are willing, we have a problem which we would like to discuss with you—"

Nate held up a hand. "After we eat. I would be a poor host if I let guests go unfed. Or have you eaten this morning?"

"We have not. We rode all night in order to overtake our father."

Winona took that as her cue. She already had a heaping stack of flapjacks done and was working on a second batch. "Each of you take one," she said, passing out china plates.

The four warriors didn't know what to do with them. Only Hunts Elk raised his to his nose and sniffed it. Humpy bit his, testing it with his teeth as he might test gold. Rabbit Tail held the one Winona gave him with two fingers, as if wary of it biting *him,* and looked around in confusion.

When Nate set his plate down, the Shoshones imitated him. From then on, they mimicked everything he did. When he placed his fork, spoon, and knife next to his plate, they did the same. When Winona brought over a tray and he selected two pancakes, each of the warriors selected two and only two. Nate covered his with syrup; they covered theirs. He cut his flapjacks into strips; they cut theirs accordingly.

Forks weren't a typical Shoshone implement, so when Nate speared a piece with his and placed it in his mouth, the four warriors awkwardly picked up theirs forks and made a few practice jabs before they began eating. Soon they were devouring the meal with keen relish and merrily smacking their lips. Not a solitary morsel was left uneaten. Under Shoshone custom, for them to do so would be rude.

The hot rolls were greeted with equal zeal. Humpy proved to be a bottomless pit, eating half again as many as everyone else.

Piping hot coffee washed everything down. As Nate sipped his, he glanced at Teeth Like A Beaver, who had eaten by the fireplace instead of joining them. "Come over here," he directed.

A full belly had improved the oldster's disposition. He complied, bestowing a haughty look on Man Without A Wife. "Whatever my good friend wants, I am more than happy to do."

"Why do you never show the same regard for us, father?" Man Without A Wife said. "Why do you make our lives miserable to satisfy your silly whim."

David Thompson

"Silly?" Teeth Like A Beaver exploded. "Is it silly to love someone with all that you are? Is it silly to miss them so much, you spend every day dreaming of them?"

"No," Man Without A Wife said, "but it *is* silly to pine after a woman who died so many winters ago. You have had three wives since Bright Morning, three wives who loved you as much as she did. Yet all you think of is her."

"Who are you to criticize me? What do you know of the love of men and women? You, who have never taken a wife and never will!"

"Father, please," Humpy said. "Do not start that again."

Teeth Like A Beaver was too mad to listen. "None of you have the right to criticize me. None of you had the right to follow me." In his fury he shook a gnarled fist. "I tell you now, I will not go back! If you force me, I will sneak away the first chance I get! If you try to bind me, I will bite your fingers off!"

Man Without A Wife wriggled his left hand, taunting his father. "Go ahead and try."

Only Hunts Elk looked at Nate. "Again you see what I must put up with. Nothing I say or do brings peace between them."

"Some people have heads of rock," Nate responded, and when Teeth Like A Beaver was about to say something to Man Without A Wife, he pounded the floor so hard his plate rattled. "No more arguing, no more fighting. You are guests in my lodge, and you will behave as guests are supposed to behave."

"As you wish, Grizzly Killer," the father said. "But it is hard for man to control himself when his own offspring shames him in front of others."

"I shame *you*—" Man Without A Wife bristled.

"You both shame yourselves," Nate declared. "I will not repeat myself again. Behave, or leave my lodge and never show yourselves in my valley again."

The pair finally clammed up.

"Before we go any further," Nate said, addressing the

sons and grandson, "there is something you must know. I have given my word I will take your father to Bear Canyon, and I hope you will not try to stop us."

"We would not think of stopping you," Only Hunts Elk said.

"What sort of trick are you playing?" Teeth Like A Beaver asked suspiciously.

"It is no trick, father. We did not come all this way to drag you back to our village. We want to help you fulfill your wish."

"Then why did you not say so sooner?"

"You did not give us the chance," Only Hunts Elk said, and elaborated. "The entire family talked it over after you ran off. We agreed that if it means this much to you, we should help you, not hinder you. So we drew sticks to see who would come and who would stay to watch over our wives and children."

"And the four of you lost," Teeth Like A Beaver said bitterly.

"The important thing is we came," Only Hunts Elk said. "We will take you to Bear Canyon, if you want. We will honor your request to lie next to Bright Morning. You need not bother Grizzly Killer."

Out of the corner of his eye, Nate observed his wife's sudden intense interest and divined why; there was no need for him to go if the others were. "What changed your minds?" he queried.

"Several things. First and foremost, he is our father, and despite all he has put us through, we care for him. When we were growing up he was always there for us. Can we do less when he needs our aid?"

Teeth Like A Beaver was dumbfounded.

"We talked long into the night," Only Hunts Elk revealed. "Two other brothers and one of our sisters thought we should turn our backs on our father. But one brother insisted it would be wrong and convinced everyone else the same."

David Thompson

"Who?" the old warrior asked. "Horn Of Hair On The Forehead? He has always been the most dependable, the most loyal. Always the one who made sure I had plenty of firewood on cold days and plenty of food to fill my belly."

"I am not at liberty to say who it was," Only Hunts Elk said. "The important thing is that we are here, and we will go with you. Grizzly Killer need not."

Nate saw Winona grin, but she didn't say anything. It was against Shoshone practice for a woman to speak when warriors were in council unless specifically asked to do so.

Nate was in a quandary. Here was a golden opportunity for him to gracefully back out of his promise without leaving Teeth Like A Beaver in the lurch. Winona clearly figured he would, but he balked at the notion. His hankering to see the grandfather of all bears was stronger than he had imagined—or had been willing to admit. "I would still like to go," Nate heard himself say, and Winona frowned and bowed her head, her long hair spilling over her face.

"We would be honored to have you," Humpy said.

"Your knowledge of bears will be of enormous help," Only Hunts Elk declared. "None of us have ever killed the great brown ones, although I did wound a male that attacked me when I was hunting antelope four winters past."

"We have all killed black bears, though," Man Without A Wife mentioned with excessive pride. "Except for Rabbit Tail. He is young, and there is much he has yet to do."

Nate glanced at the youth, who hadn't let out a peep since entering the cabin. "How do you feel about all this?"

Like the women, younger men were not permitted to speak unless invited by someone older. Rabbit Tail smiled at the honor Nate had done him and answered, "I want to help my grandfather. When I was little he taught me how to use a bow, and when my pony was stolen by the Crows,

54

he gave me another. Whatever I can do to repay him, I will. I have wanted to all along."

Teeth Like A Beaver smirked at Only Hunts Elk. "Do you hear your son? How sad that my grandson is more honorable than those I brought into this world."

"He does not have a wife and four children of his own to take care of," Only Hunts Elk responded. "I could not simply up and leave when you first told us what you had in mind."

"Excuses. Always excuses," Teeth Like A Beaver said.

"If you ask me," Man Without A Wife piped up, "bringing Rabbit Tail was a mistake. He has never counted coup, never proven himself. Yet you expect him to hold his own against the grandfather of all bears."

Only Hunts Elk did not like having his son insulted. "Maybe Rabbit Tail has never slain an enemy, but he is one of the best hunters in the tribe. And he has never run from a challenge. My son will prove worthy. Wait and see."

"I sincerely hope so," Man Without A Wife said. "It is one thing to lose a foolish father, another to lose my favorite nephew."

Humpy posed a question none of the others had thought to ask. "When do you plan to leave, Grizzly Killer?"

"At first light," Nate replied, and when he did, Winona was up and out the door in a twinkling. "Excuse me," he said, hastening after her. She was almost to the trees, her fists clenched at her sides, and he couldn't tell if she was mad or sad until he overtook her and heard soft sobs that ended the second she sensed him. "What's the matter?" he inquired in English.

"Need you ask?"

"I gave my word," Nate stressed.

"It is not like you to try to deceive me."

Nate put a hand on her shoulder, but Winona shrugged it off. "I'll have Zach and Louisa come down and stay with you until I get back. You'll be perfectly safe."

"That is not the issue," Winona said.

"What is?"

"It is not like you to act ignorant, either."

"I told you I want to visit Bear Canyon. Whether I take Teeth Like A Beaver myself or with the others is irrelevant. If the whole tribe offered to escort him, I'd still want to see the canyon for myself."

"And if I ask you not to go?"

"Don't do this to me, Winona. I love you more than life itself, and I would never deliberately hurt you. Not in a million years."

"Then stay."

"I can't. Anyway, you haven't given me a good reason."

"That I don't want you to isn't reason enough? There was a time when what I desired was important."

"Why is it women always twist words around to suit them?"

"Why is it men always ignore words when it suits them?"

Winona turned, and for a second Nate thought she would give him a tongue-lashing, but she only wrapped her arms around him and hugged him close. "I'm awful sorry if I've upset you," he said. "But you should look at the bright side."

"There is one?"

"You won't have to worry with the other warriors along. There's safety in numbers."

"Teeth Like A Beaver's father probably thought the same thing and look at what happened to him and his party." Winona gripped his chin in both her hands. "I have a bad feeling about this, husband. A very bad feeling. If I thought it would change your mind, I would yell and cry like other women do."

"I'll be fine. A year from now we'll look back on this day and laugh at how silly it was to fret so much."

"Who among us can predict tomorrow? Taking life for

56

granted is as unwise as courting danger. None of us are immune to harm. The Great Mystery does not have favorites. Each dawn brings with it the promise of life and the threat of death." Winona kissed him. "Do not deprive me of all the dawns we have yet to share."

Nate was deeply touched by her affection, and he almost gave in. Almost. "I still have to do it."

Winona held him a good long while. When she stepped back, she was composed and calm. "Very well. We all do what we must."

On that enigmatic note they returned to the cabin.

Teeth Like A Beaver was showing his family the stone fireplace and crowing about the comfortable night's sleep he'd had.

Rabbit Tail, though, was more interested in the rocking chair. Evelyn was rocking back and forth while singing to her doll, and the young Shoshone had hunkered to examine the curved slats at the bottom. He stood when Nate and Winona entered and stepped back as if in fear he had done something wrong.

To Nate's mild surprise, Winona made no further mention of his impending trek. He spent the afternoon shoeing the black stallion. After sunset he packed, then cleaned and oiled his rifle and pistols.

Only Hunts Elk asked permission to build a fire in the clearing, and Nate consented. The Shoshones spent the evening huddled around the crackling flames, Teeth Like A Beaver included.

Nate visited with them for a spell. They were jawing about yesteryear, about the frolics and tragedies their family had experienced. Even Man Without A Wife was in a pleasant mood for once, and no arguments broke out.

Bear Canyon was never mentioned. By an unspoken common consent, the subject was taboo. They were all aware of the gravity of their undertaking and no one wanted to be reminded of the potential horrors ahead. For this one evening they ate and joked and laughed, old grudges forgotten, old prejudices buried.

Nate went inside at eight. Along about nine Evelyn came to the table where he was sharpening his Green River knife, and climbed up onto his lap. He didn't object. Setting down the whetstone and cloth, he said, "Something on your mind, little one?"

"I just want to spend some time with you before you go, Pa. You'll be gone a long time, Ma says."

"A month at the most," Nate guessed. According to Teeth Like A Beaver, it would take nine or ten days of hard riding to reach Bear Canyon. Another ten or so would be consumed in the ride back. How many days were in between depended on how long the old warrior took to meet his Maker. Teeth Like A Beaver insisted it wouldn't be long. In fact, he had promised Nate to "fall over dead" the moment they found the shelf where Bright Morning had been buried.

Winona was at the counter, filling a parfleche with pemmican and jerky. "Will one be enough, husband?"

"One should do me right fine," Nate said.

"Do you have your fire steel and flint?"

"Of course." Nate patted the possibles bag that was always slung across his chest along with his powder horn and ammo pouch. He never went anywhere without them. Neither did any other mountaineer, a legacy of lessons learned during the heyday of the beaver trade. "You ought to know by now I would never leave home without them."

"Are you taking your tomahawk?"

"Naturally."

"Your spyglass?"

"Got that, too. Why all these questions?"

"I do not want you to go off unprepared," Winona said with a meaningful glance at their daughter.

Evelyn lightly pulled on Nate's beard. "You will be careful, won't you, Pa?"

"Always."

"Want to play checkers?"

For the next hour Nate did exactly that, two games with his daughter and then a game against his wife at Evelyn's request.

Winona wasn't as talkative as she normally would be, added proof, as if any were needed, of how upset she was. She played well, but then Winona did most everything well. Nate never failed to be impressed by her remarkable knack for learning new things. She soaked up information like a sponge soaked up water. Years ago, she had beaten him the second time she ever played checkers. Tonight, she beat him for the umpteenth time, much to Evelyn's delight.

Afterward they tucked Evelyn in. Nate ventured outdoors, where the Shoshones were still chattering like chipmunks. Teeth Like A Beaver announced that he would sleep outside to be with his sons and grandson. Nate bid them goodnight.

Winona had already turned back the quilts on their bed. Nate barred the door, blew out the lamps, and climbed in with her, pulling the curtain closed for privacy's sake. In light of how she had been treating him all day, he was taken aback when she rolled over and molded her body to his.

Dawn arrived much too soon. Nate sat up, yawning, sluggish from only a couple of hours sleep, and walked barefoot to the fireplace to stoke the embers. Dressing, he stepped outside to saddle the stallion.

The Shoshones were up and waiting, their mounts bridled, their demeanor somber. Gone was the gaiety, the laughter.

Nate didn't have much of an appetite, but at Winona's insistence he downed a buttered roll. Their parting was brief. Wife and daughter hugged and kissed him, and that was it. No tears. No protests.

Forking leather, Nate gave a flick of the reins and rode northward, his destination Bear Canyon—and the unknown.

Chapter Five

"Grizzly Killer, we are being followed!" Rabbit Tail hollered.

Nate King shifted in his saddle and gazed along the row of warriors to the last in line. The youth was pointing to the south, where a pair of riders had emerged from dense pines and were crossing a grassy tract. A tract Nate and the Shoshones had crossed a short while ago. There could be no doubt the two riders were shadowing them.

From his possibles bag Nate took a small collapsible spyglass he had obtained in trade at a rendezvous years ago. Unfolding it, he trained it on the pair. Not that he needed to. He knew who they were, and he wasn't the only one.

"Is it who I think it is?" Only Hunts Elk asked.

"Afraid so," Nate said, lowering the telescope. Replacing it, he rode on, climbing a switchback sprinkled with tall firs and stands of aspens. In another hundred yards he came to a stand of pines in deep shadow and drew rein, announcing, "This is as good a spot as any. We will wait for them."

Only Hunts Elk reined up next to him. "What will you do?"

"Try to convince them to go back," Nate said.

Teeth Like A Beaver was staring down the mountain. "I hope they will listen. This is the same thing that happened to me, and I lost Bright Morning as a result." He slid a leg over the sorrel. "Why is it women never do as we ask them? As old as I am, as many wives as I have had, and I still do not understand how they think."

"No man does," Humpy said.

"I once had a friend who claimed he did," Teeth Like A Beaver said. "He bragged about it all the time, and crowed how no woman would ever get the better of him. Then he took a wife who insulted him in public, made him do woman's work around the lodge, and hit him when he did not do as she wanted. My friend would have been better off marrying a porcupine."

"He did not know as much about women as he thought he did," Only Hunts Elk commented.

"I believe most females mean well," Teeth Like A Beaver said. "But they cannot help being strange. They are born that way."

For the next forty minutes the warriors discussed the opposite gender, Nate listening with half an ear. He was more interested in the two riders. It was doubtful the pair were aware he had called a halt. Unwittingly, they were riding right into his hands.

"When I was younger I thought women were better than men," Teeth Like A Beaver was reminiscing. "I saw them as sweeter, kinder, gentler. Then I noticed how they like to complain about everything, how nothing a man ever does pleases them, how some of them nag and nag and nag some more, and I realized they have two faces. One for when a man does things as they want them done, and one for when he does not."

61

"And one face for when they are out among others, and one for when they are alone with their men," Only Hunts Elk said.

"That makes four faces," Man Without A Wife noted.

"They also have a face for when they are with their own relatives and another face for when they are with their husband's relatives," Humpy said.

"Six faces now." Teeth Like A Beaver sighed. "No wonder they can never make up their minds about anything."

The warriors burst into hearty mirth, but Nate did not join in. The two riders were only a few hundred feet below, and the lead rider had straightened and was looking right at the cluster of trees that screened them. She knew.

Rising, Nate walked into the open and waited with his arms folded. He should have been mad, but he wasn't. She wasn't the type to stay home gnawing her nails in anxiety when her man was in possible peril. It was too much to expect, and he said as much as soon as they came within earshot.

Winona was leading a pack horse. She wore a plainer, heavier dress and a red shawl. A Hawken was in the crook of her left arm, and a pair of flintlocks were at her waist. "Then you should not hold this against me, husband," she said in English.

"Howdy, Pa," Evelyn said cheerfully. "Did we surprise you? Ma told me to keep it a secret."

"She did, did she?"

"We packed yesterday when you were busy shoeing your horse and hid the packs in the root cellar." Evelyn giggled. "We were set to go before you were." Instead of one of her fashionable dresses, she wore a buckskin dress patterned like her mother's. Her custom-made Hawken was across her saddle.

"You sure hoodwinked me," Nate said.

"To spare us hours of useless argument," Winona remarked, bringing her mare to a stop, "and before you start another, keep one thing in mind: If you will not listen to reason, why should I?"

Nate tilted his head toward Evelyn.

"I have a solution," Winona said. "We will leave her with Zach and Lou. She is looking forward to it."

"Louisa is a lot of fun," Evelyn declared. "She's the next best thing to having my very own sister."

The Shoshones filed from the firs, Teeth Like A Beaver grinning wide enough to show his oversized teeth. "We might as well take her along, Grizzly Killer. Trying to change a woman's mind after it is made up is like trying to change the course of a river in full flood."

Winona arched an eyebrow. "Oh, is it really? Men are no better. Trying to reason with them is like trying to reason with a tree stump."

"You would get along great with my wife," Humpy said. "She has the same high opinion of men that you do."

Nate could see that trying to convince his wife would be impossible. "We might as well head out," he said, pivoting. "I want to reach my son's lodge by midday tomorrow."

They mounted up. Nate assumed the lead, Winona and Evelyn on either side, the warriors strung out in their wake. The sun was at its zenith when they reached the top of the mountain and started down the other side.

"Are you upset with me?" Winona finally came right out and inquired.

"Upset, no. But a little disappointed."

"No more so than I was with you. I have not asked for much during the course of our marriage, and when you refused, I felt as if a knife had been plunged into my heart."

Nate winced as if a knife had been buried in his. "I'm sorry. Truly sorry. It will never happen again."

"Never say never, husband," Winona advised. "Life makes liars of us when we do."

The rest of the day was largely uneventful. Late in the

afternoon they flushed out a pair of blacktail bucks that bounded off in long leaps. Humpy and Man Without A Wife were eager to take after them, but Nate objected to wasting the daylight that remained. They forged on until twilight and pitched camp beside a gurgling stream.

Nate and Rabbit Tail went hunting for something for the supper pot. A squirrel chittered at them, but Nate dismissed it as too puny. When a rabbit streaked from cover, Nate held his fire in the hope of bagging a bigger animal.

On a hill adjacent to the stream they found a game trail. Abundant tracks confirmed deer and elk used it regularly, so Nate led the youth into nearby brush. He didn't think they would have long to wait.

Minutes dragged by. Rabbit Tail sat as motionless as a statue, his ash bow in his left hand, an arrow nocked to the sinew string.

The shadows lengthened. In a little while it would be too dark to shoot reliably. Nate was debating whether to give up the still hunt and rove through the undergrowth when without warning a four-legged apparition materialized on the trail a mere ten yards from their hiding place. He heard Rabbit Tail's sudden intake of breath, and so did the animal.

It was a mountain lion, a large, sleek tawny male, steely muscles rippling as it glided down the trail with its small head lower than its body and its long tail twitching like a serpent. At Rabbit Tail's gasp, the big cat froze, its tail straight out, its nostrils twitching as it tested the air for scent. Suddenly its tail jerked up and the cougar executed a tremendous leap, bounding toward the opposite side of the trail, hurtling twelve to fifteen feet.

As quick as the mountain lion was, Nate was faster. He fixed a hasty bead when the beast was in midair and stroked the Hawken's trigger. The ball caught the cat low in the ribs and ranged up through its chest, the impact tumbling it in a whirl of limbs and tail until it came to rest against the bole of a tree.

Springing up, Nate drew a pistol and rushed toward it, prepared to finish it off if need be. Rabbit Tail never left his side, the bow string drawn all the way back.

The predator started to rise.

"You do the honors," Nate said.

Without hesitation Rabbit Tail loosed his shaft, and the barbed point sliced high into the cougar's body. It uttered a feral growl that ended in a strangled cry. Blood gushing from its nostrils and mouth, it collapsed and convulsed, then was still.

Nate nudged the mountain lion with a toe, and when there was no reaction, he cautiously hunkered to verify the big cat was done for. It never paid to take anything for granted. A few summers ago a pair of Flatheads had stumbled on a cougar and felled it with a shot from a fusee, a trade rifle. Dismounting, they had rushed over to collect their trophy. But the hunters became the hunted when the lion galvanized to life and sprang. It killed one warrior and chased the other to his horse. The man had been lucky to get out of there with his life.

"Is it dead?" Rabbit Tail asked, another arrow notched.

"We have our supper," Nate said, grinning. Painter meat was a favorite among the mountaineering fraternity. Many rated it tastier than venison or elk or even buffalo. Owing to the reclusive, elusive nature of cougars, however, the opportunity to partake of one were few and far between.

Nate went looking for a suitable pole and found a fallen branch that would suffice. Drawing his tomahawk, he trimmed it, then slid it between the cat's front and rear legs. Since he had not brought his rope along, he had to make do, and did so by cutting enough whangs from his buckskin shirt to tie the cougar to the pole. Most Easterners didn't know the fringe on buckskin was for more than decoration.

Rabbit Tail was beaming with pride. For a hunter to slay a cougar was rare, and his standing would rise among his people once word spread. As they hoisted the cat, he said sincerely, "Thank you, Grizzly Killer. I will never forget your kindness."

Guided by a flickering point of light, they made a bee-line for camp. The horses had been hobbled for the night, and Winona and Evelyn were at the stream filling a coffee pot with water.

Rabbit Tail let out with a yip that brought the other warriors on the run. Excitedly gathered around, they examined the cat, comparing it to others they had seen. Rabbit Tail related how he had finished it off and the older men congratulated him, Humpy clapping the youth on the back.

Only Hunts Elk was happiest of all. "You did well, son!" he exclaimed as the lion was deposited a goodly distance from the horses to avoid spooking them. "Only one other warrior in our village has ever slain one."

Rabbit Tail drew his hunting knife. "Since you shot first, Grizzly Killer, the skin is yours."

"I have no use for it," Nate said. "You can keep it."

"That would not be right," Rabbit Tail said. Although, judging by his expression, he coveted the hide as much as whites coveted gold.

"It would if you earned it," Nate said. "I want to spend time with my wife and daughter. So if you do the butchering, the skin is yours."

"I am in your debt again," Rabbit Tail said, and eagerly bent to the task. Rolling the lion over, he inserted the tip of the tapered blade midway between its two rear legs and carefully cut upward.

Nate started to walk off, but Only Hunts Elk gripped his wrist and mouthed the words, "Thank you."

Teeth Like A Beaver fell into step beside Nate as he walked toward the fire. "You are as generous as you are brave, Grizzly Killer. The more I know of you, the more I like you."

"Don't make more of it than it is. I already have the

skin of a long-tail cat at my lodge," Nate said. "Long-tail cat" was what the Shoshones called mountain lions to distinguish them from bobcats and lynx. "What use would another be?"

"Belittle your kindness all you want but you do not fool me." Teeth Like A Beaver grew thoughtful. "Since you are the first white man I have known, I must ask. Are all whites as you are?"

"No. No two people, white or red, are ever alike. Some whites are friendly; some are not. Just as some Indians are friendly and some are hostile."

Winona had coffee brewing and was rummaging in a parfleche. "I remember putting a canister of sugar in this bag," she said in English. "Ah." She held it out, the firelight playing over its floral pattern. "Thank goodness. I know how grumpy you get when you do not start your day with your morning coffee."

"I'm not that bad," Nate said.

"No worse than a grizzly fresh out of hibernation," Winona responded, at which Evelyn cackled.

"Ma is telling the truth, Pa. Sometimes you're like a snarly old bear until you've had your coffee. Zach used to say maybe we should feed it to real bears and they wouldn't be so mean."

Teeth Like A Beaver was at a total loss. "What did they say, my friend?" he asked.

"That you are welcome to join us," Nate replied in Shoshone and was roundly laughed at by his wife and daughter.

"You're terrible, Pa," Evelyn said.

Winona reached up and clasped Nate's calloused hand. "You are a bad influence, husband. If you are not careful, our daughter will think it is perfectly all right to go around fibbing."

"It isn't?" Nate bantered, easing onto a short log someone had dragged there for that purpose. "And if *you're* not careful, you'll have our daughter thinking all women like to poke fun at their husbands."

"They don't?" Winona held her own.

Teeth Like A Beaver was, if nothing else, blunt. Lowering onto his haunches, he said, fittingly enough, "I have been meaning to ask your wife a question, Grizzly Killer, if you do not mind." He faced Winona. "Do not take offense, but do you like being the wife of a white man?"

"I love Grizzly Killer with all my heart."

"He is a good husband?"

"No woman could ask for better. In twenty winters he has never beaten me, never bullied me, never forced me to do anything against my will. I have only to ask and he will do his utmost to get me anything I desire."

"It sounds as if he loves you as much as I loved Bright Morning. I would have gladly died in her stead that day."

To take the old man's mind off it, Nate said, "Tell me more about the canyon. How big is it? What other animals live there beside the big bears?"

"They are not big, they are *giant*." Teeth Like A Beaver corrected him. "As for the canyon, it is no wider than the distance five arrows can fly, one after the other."

A skilled archer, as Nate had witnessed many times, could send an arrow a hundred yards, give or take. Five arrows, therefore, equaled five hundred yards. Not wide at all, he mused.

"It is difficult to say how long the canyon is. There are too many twists and turns," Teeth Like A Beaver related. "My guess would be that it is half as long as the distance from where Beaver Creek flows into the Little Wind River to Wind River itself."

Nate was familiar with that area. Both the rendezvous of 1830 and 1838 had been held on a nearby plain. To the best of his recollection, it was about four miles from the junction of Beaver Creek and Little Wind River to Wind River. Which meant Bear Canyon was two miles long.

"We saw deer sign and elk," the old Shoshone said. "Birds, of course. The usual small game. But at night we heard things we had never heard before, cries and howls of creatures we could not identify. And once, just before dawn, when I was keeping watch, I saw something in the brush on the other side of the stream. It was too small to be the grandfather of all bears, and yet it was bigger than a horse."

"You have no idea what it was?"

Teeth Like A Beaver glanced toward the slain mountain lion. "From the way it moved, I thought it might be a cat. But if so, it had the longest teeth of any cat that ever lived. Two of the upper ones were as long as my hand."

"Gosh!" Evelyn exclaimed. "I would like to see a cat like that."

So would Nate, but he didn't want her around when he did. Nor, for that matter, did he want Winona on hand. Persuading her to stay with Zach, though, would be next to impossible.

"The cries were the worst," Teeth Like A Beaver had gone on. "They brought goose bumps to my skin and set my teeth to chattering."

"Can you describe them?" Winona asked.

"I can try. Have you ever heard the scream of a long-tail cat in the still of night?"

"Who hasn't?" Nate said.

"Then imagine a cry ten times louder, ten times shriller, ten times more fierce, a cry torn from the throat of a creature more savage than a hungry grizzly and more vicious than a rampaging wolverine."

Nate tried but couldn't. The screams of painters were bad enough. A cry ten times worse seemed beyond the pale of possibility.

"There was a flying thing, too, I think," Teeth Like A Beaver revealed. "I heard it in the darkness, the flap of huge wings passing overheard. I dropped onto my back with my lance pointed at the sky but all I saw was a large shape. Maybe the fire scared it off. I can not say."

"Could there be people there?" Evelyn said. "Living in the canyon, I mean?"

"Perhaps, young one, although I do not see how. They would fall prey to the grandfather of all bears or the giant cat or the other things I heard."

"Maybe the people are just as fierce as the animals," Evelyn said.

Nate hoped not. His plan was to sneak in and sneak out unnoticed. Evading the huge bears and whatever else inhabited the canyon would be difficult enough. He didn't need the added worry of contending with hostiles.

To the west a coyote yipped and was answered by another to the south. Somewhere close by an owl was posing the eternal query of its kind. A minute later a wolf howled, a lonesome, wavering call that wafted on the stiff wind like the eerie wail of a soul in torment. Sounds Nate was accustomed to. Sounds of the world as it should be, not filled with monstrous demons from the dawn of time.

In due course the coffee was done, and Winona handed Nate his battered tin cup filled to the brim. They made small talk about whether the good weather would hold, about the prospects of encountering Blackfeet, which were slim, or the Crows, which were not so slim.

Only Hunts Elk came over with a sizeable chunk of cougar meat skewered on a makeshift spit and rigged it over the fire. The tantalizing aroma of roasting meat filled the night.

"Mmmm," Evelyn said. "I'm so hungry my belly is growling."

As if on cue, so did something else, something off in the trees. Nate jumped to his feet, his Hawken in hand. Winona and the warriors rose, too, clutching their weapons.

"Is it a griz, Pa?" Evelyn asked.

Nate merely nodded. The growl was repeated, closer this time. A twig snapped with a loud crack.

"Will it attack, you think?" Teeth Like A Beaver whispered.

If it did, it could wreak havoc. Nate sidled toward their tethered mounts. Bears usually went after the horses, and they could ill afford to lose a single one. From the noise the beast was making, it had to be a young one. Older silver-tips were much more cautious, much more quiet. They attacked from ambush, without warning, giving their quarry no chance to fight back or flee.

Man Without A Wife was also moving toward the horses, his lance extended. "Will it rush us, Grizzly Killer?" he wondered.

"There is no telling," Nate said. Bears in general, and grizzles in particular, were the most unpredictable creatures on God's green earth. Where one might run at the sight of a human, another would track a man for miles for the express purpose of devouring him.

"If it does, what do we do? I have never fought a brown bear before."

"I will try to bring it down with my rifle and pistols," Nate said. Which wasn't guaranteed to work. Grizzly skulls were so thick and broad, most balls glanced off without effect. Heart and lung shots fared little better thanks to a bear's massive bulk. There had been instances where more than a dozen shots were needed to slay one grizzly. Years ago, Meriwether Lewis of the famed Lewis and Clark expedition had written that grizzlies were "hard to die." Truer words, as the old saw had it, had never been penned.

A grunt issued from the brush. By now the horses were well aware of the threat and were nickering and prancing in fright. All except the black stallion, which stood with its head high, its ears pricked. The stallion's calmness in the face of danger was one of the major reasons Nate relied on it. There was nothing worse than having a mount bolt in the heat of battle, which was why warriors valued their war horses more than any other, some going so far as to keep prized animals inside their lodges at night so enemies couldn't steal them.

"Look!" Rabbit Tail yelled.

Nate saw them, too, a pair of eyes gleaming at the edge of the firelight. From their size and height, he was more sure than ever the grizzly was young. The bear was uncertain whether it wanted to charge. The fire, the strange scents, were keeping it at bay. At any moment, though, it might make up its mind, and all hell would break loose.

Drawing a pistol, Nate declared, "Be ready! I am going to try and drive it off!"

"By shooting it?" Man Without A Wife said skeptically.

Nate didn't blame him. Wounded bears frequently went berserk with fury and would tear the person who wounded them to ribbons. "No," he answered, and pointed the muzzle at the ground.

"It is coming closer!" Rabbit Tail warned.

That it was, but slowly, warily, looking from the horses to the fire. Nate thumbed back the hammer, then let out with a strident whoop while simultaneously squeezing the trigger.

At the blast, the grizzly snorted and wheeled. In another moment it was barreling into the forest, crashing through everything in its path. The din of its departure gradually faded, and the night was quiet again.

Man Without A Wife laughed. "Your reputation is well deserved, Grizzly Killer. You knew just what to do."

The other warriors were likewise elated. Humpy joked about the bear having the courage of a rabbit.

Winona, though, summed it up best. "We were lucky, husband."

"That we were."

"Let us hope we are just as lucky if we meet up with the grandfather of all bears."

Chapter Six

GONE HUNTING. The two words scrawled on the note tacked to the door of Zachary King's cabin said it all. "Damn," Nate King declared and swung from the saddle to confirm his son was gone.

Locks were as rare as hen's teeth on the frontier. Doors and windows could be barred or bolted from the inside, but at any other time anyone could walk on in. Nate entered and surveyed the immaculate interior. A female touch was very much in evidence. Zach's wife had hung pink curtains on the windows and draped a pink tablecloth over their big oak table. A store-bought rug in front of the fireplace, a doily on a small reading table, and a tapestry on a wall were also Lousia's handiwork.

Nate backed out and closed the door. Winona had translated the note for the benefit of the Shoshones, and Teeth Like A Beaver framed Nate's dilemma in a question.

"What do we with your daughter now, Grizzly Killer?"

Nate looked at his wife and said in English, "I suppose

73

I'd be wasting my breath if I asked you to stay here with her?"

"You would."

"Be sensible."

"I recall saying the same to you at our cabin and you refused."

"This is different. It's Evelyn we're talking about, not me."

Winona switched to her own tongue. "With our son gone, what else would you have us do? Abandon our daughter? We are a family, husband. We have come this far together, we will go the rest of the way together."

Nate was willing to debate her until doomsday, if that was what it took to convince her, but Only Hunts Elk picked that moment to climb down and come over.

"May I speak with you alone, Grizzly Killer?"

They moved off toward the wood shed, and the stocky warrior turned so his back was to the rest. "We each have a similar problem, Grizzly Killer. Maybe we can help each other solve them."

"My ears are open."

"I know how stubborn wives can be. If yours wants to go, there is little you can do other than tie her up and leave her here. And you do not impress me as the kind to do something like that."

"No, I am not," Nate agreed. Although, truth to tell, the notion had its appeal.

Only Hunts Elk lowered his voice. "I never wanted Rabbit Tail to come along, either. He is too young, too inexperienced. But at our family council, when it came time to draw sticks, I could not refuse his request to take part or I would have shamed him in the eyes of our entire family."

"I understand."

"I have not been able to think of a way to keep my son from going into Bear Canyon with us without offending him. Until now."

74

"I have lost your trail."

"Neither you nor you wife want to expose your daughter to danger, but you are caught in a bind. The same as I. The solution is to combine the two. You must refuse to take your daughter into Bear Canyon, and when you do, I will offer to have Rabbit Tail watch over her while we are gone. Both your daughter and my son would be out of danger, and both of us will have one less worry."

Nate smiled. He liked the idea, liked it a lot. The only alternative was to take Evelyn on to Shakespeare McNair's, which would add another five or six days to their journey. And Evelyn should be perfectly safe with Rabbit Tail. Green though he was, the youth had demonstrated grit and savvy.

"What do you say, Grizzly Killer?"

"You are as clever as a fox, Only Hunts Elk. We will do as you suggest. At the right moment, I will bring it up."

No one showed any interest in what they had discussed except Winona. "What did you talk about, husband?" she asked in English.

"I'll tell you later," Nate said, hoping she would forget to bring it up.

"Very well. Just so you were not conniving."

"Me?"

"All men are connivers. Some just hide it better than others."

On that flattering note, Nate stepped into the stirrups and they cantered to the northwest. That night their meal consisted of leftover cougar. They slept undisturbed by roving beasts, and were on the go again as a rosy crown rimmed the eastern horizon.

Day after day it was more of the same. Long, hard hours in the saddle. Slumber under the stars. Game was abundant, so they never lacked for food. Twice they spotted grizzlies but at a distance.

Once they accidentally flushed a small herd of shaggy

mountain buffalo in dense timber and an irate bull challenged them by barring their path and stomping the ground. Nate had no desire to shoot the bull if he could avoid it. Most of the meat would go to waste, and they wouldn't be able to cure the hide. So he was relieved when the brute huffed off on the heels of the cows.

Teeth Like A Beaver became more and more excited with each passing sunset. He rode at the head of their column, always on the lookout for landmarks. Whenever he spied one, he would yell and flap his arms in glee.

The countryside underwent a change. The forested slopes and verdant valleys gave way to rocky, dry terrain crisscrossed by ravines and gullies and dotted by stark spires and misshapen hills. The contrast was startling, akin to venturing into a whole new world, an alien realm where Nature was warped and stunted. Wildlife was scarce. Nate reckoned that animals shunned the region due to the lack of water. But he could not help thinking that maybe there was another, more sinister, reason.

"We are getting close!" Teeth Like A Beaver announced on their ninth day out. "Another sleep and we should reach the entrance. I only hope the opening is still there."

"It is not too late to change your mind, father," Man Without A Wife said.

The pair had not spatted in over a week, and Nate had almost forgotten how they were always at each other's throats. Now the father rounded on his son with surprising resentment, stabbing a finger at him.

"You would like that, wouldn't you? Everyone in our village would grin and say you were right. I must be touched in the head. Why else did I give up when I was so close?"

"No one will think less of you."

"Wrong. *I* will think less of me. My love for Bright Morning would mean nothing if I turned back now. I am

76

seeing this through to the end, and nothing you say or do will dissuade me."

That evening they camped on a high bluff. Several thousand feet below lay a vast lowland that stretched as far as the eye could see to the north and south.

Nate hunted for over an hour without spying a single animal, so jerky and pemmican had to suffice for their supper. The warriors were all uncommonly quiet. Along about ten, as Nate was checking on the horses prior to turning in, Teeth Like A Beaver ambled up.

"Tomorrow is the day I have waited over seventy winters for, Grizzly Killer. In case I do not have the chance later, I want to thank you again for agreeing to help. No matter what happens, you have done me a great kindness."

"I just hope we can find the shelf," Nate said.

Teeth Like A Beaver gazed toward the forms by the fire. "One other thing, my friend. Something for you to consider." He paused. "Were it my wife and daughter, I would not let them enter Bear Canyon. Having lost Bright Morning, having seen the horrors I have seen, I would do whatever was necessary to stop Winona and Blue Flower. Do you understand? *Whatever was necessary.*"

"I will do what I can."

"That is not enough. You must be strong. You must be firm. For if you are not, many winters from now you will look back and regret you did not heed my advice. Regret it more than you can ever know."

Deep in thought, Nate strolled to the end of the bluff. He listened but heard nothing. Absolutely nothing at all. No coyotes, no wolves, no painters, no owls. The benighted lowland was eerily empty of life. Or so he thought until a faint cry reached his ears. Faint, yet disturbing, in that it was a cry he did not recognize. A shriek that undulated on and on, like the screech of a banshee, then abruptly ended.

Nate wondered if he were biting off more than he could chew. If maybe, in his overriding urge to see Bear

Canyon, he would be pitted against creatures from which there was no escape.

A warm hand slipped into his. "What are you doing out here by yourself, husband?"

"Thinking."

"About what?"

"About how much I love you. About how devastated I will be if anything happens to you. You are my life, Winona."

"I am touched, but I am still going with you."

"You'll make it harder on me. I can't watch your back and mine at the same time."

"Then I will watch your back for you." Winona leaned against him. "Put yourself in my moccasins. I would not want to go on living if I lost you. If we must die, let it be together rather than years apart. Look at how miserable Teeth Like A Beaver has been all this time."

"I'd rather you didn't die at all," Nate said.

"I will strive my utmost not to. But know that if I do, I will pass onto the next world with no regrets. It is my choice to go with you, and I will accept the consequences."

"Stubborn wench."

"Muleheaded man."

Laughing lightly, they embraced, and Nate kissed her on the ear. "You better not let anything happen to you. I would never forgive myself."

From out the vast void below wavered the same shrill shriek as before, not quite as faint this time, a bestial challenge issuing from the depths of the dark and shrouded in the mists of mystery.

Nate felt Winona stiffen.

"What was that?"

"I can tell you what it *wasn't*. It wasn't any animal we've ever seen or heard. And whatever it is, I hope to heaven we don't run into it."

Winona shivered, but whether from the stiff breeze or

something else, Nate wasn't sure. "Let's go back," she proposed.

The Shoshones were gathered around the fire, as somber a lot as ever lived. Teeth Like A Beaver had his arms wrapped around his knees and was gazing into the flames. Man Without A Wife was sharpening his lance, Humpy was honing a knife. Only Hunts Elk was inspecting each of his two dozen arrows.

Evelyn had curled onto her side and was sound asleep. Nate picked her up without waking her, and after Winona spread out their blankets, he gently laid Evelyn down and covered her.

As Nate squatted by the fire, Only Hunts Elk caught his eye, then surreptitiously nodded at Rabbit Tail. Nate got the message and turned to his wife. "The truth is," he casually said in the Shoshone language, "I do not mind you coming along nearly so much as I do Evelyn. She is too young for this. If only we had somewhere safe where she could stay until we were done."

"We cannot help it our son was not home," Winona said.

Only Hunts Elk played it as casually as Nate. "Perhaps I could make a suggestion, Grizzly Killer? As a father I sympathize. So why not have your daughter stay outside the canyon with my son? He would be happy to watch over her."

Rabbit Tail glanced up. "What did you say, father?"

Nate gestured. "I would not want to impose."

"We would be privileged to help," Only Hunts Elk said.

The young Shoshone disagreed. "I would rather go with the rest of you, father."

"I know, son," Only Hunts Elk said. "But you owe Grizzly Killer a favor. He let you finish off the long-tail cat. He gave you the hide. Now he needs help, and you would deny him?"

Rabbit Tail's features rippled as he wrestled with his conscience. "Grandfather, what would you do?"

Teeth Like A Beaver stirred. "Grizzly Killer is your friend, and friends help friends in need."

"Think of the great trust he places in you," Only Hunts Elk said. "The life of his only daughter will be in your hands. He can do you no greater honor."

Succumbing to a twinge of guilt at how they had manipulated the youngster, Nate said, "But only if you want to do it, Rabbit Tail. If you would rather be with your father and uncles, I would understand."

Just then Evelyn rolled over and mumbled in her sleep, her face angelic in the firelight, a living portrait of all that was innocent and pure.

Rabbit Tail stared at her a few seconds, then said softly: "My father is right. You do honor me, Grizzly Killer. I will guard your daughter while you are in Bear Canyon. I will protect her with my life."

"Let us hope it does not come to that."

Everyone turned in early in order to get an early start, but Nate couldn't sleep. His mind raced with images of ravening giant bears and other nightmares, products of his overwrought imagination. Winona's head was nestled on his shoulder, and he thought she was asleep. But when he idly stroked her hair, she put her mouth to his ear and whispered.

"The two of you handled that quite well."

"What are you talking about?"

"Did I fall from the sky with the last rain? Only Hunts Elk and you had that planned ever since we stopped at Zach's."

"Don't you get tired of always knowing everything?" Nate pecked her forehead. "You're not mad, are you?"

"Mad that you put our daughter's safety above all else?" Winona grinned. "If you had not thought of something, I intended to wait outside the canyon with her."

"You did?"

"Honestly, husband. Did you really think I would expose our daughter to beasts such as Teeth Like A Beaver

80

has described? I may be stubborn, but I am not stupid. I have devoted too many years to the welfare of my family to lose my daughter over one of your ridiculous whims."

Nate couldn't decide which bothered him more. The fact his wife thought he was being ridiculous, or realizing that if he hadn't conspired with Only Hunts Elk to trick Rabbit Tail, he would have gotten what he wanted all along, and both Winona and Evelyn would have stayed out of Bear Canyon.

"Do not get me wrong, husband. From what I hear from other wives, compared to most men you are exceptional. You do not drink to excess. You do not go off with your friends for days or weeks at a time. You are a good provider."

"But?" Nate prompted when she stopped.

"But like most men you have never quite grown up. So when you hear of a place like Bear Canyon and a creature like the grandfather of all bears, you want to rush off and see them for yourself."

"You have to understand. I was raised in New York City. The only wild animals I ever saw were birds and squirrels and an occasional deer. The only exciting places I knew of were those I read about in books. The jungles of deepest Africa, the Amazon in South America, the wilds of India. As a boy I dreamed of exploring them one day, of having thrilling adventures like those I read about."

Winona chuckled. "See? You never grew up." Her lips brushed his neck. "But I would not have you any other way. You fill my heart with joy."

"Glad I do something right," Nate muttered.

"Remind me to tell you some time of the other old legends my people have. Of the lake high in the mountains where a water horse lives—"

"A *water* horse?"

"They say it has a head like a horse, yes, but it has paddles instead of legs and it eats flesh instead of grass.

81

The lake is bad medicine, and my people have not gone near it in more winters than any of us can remember."

"And you know where this lake is?"

"I could find it if I had to. When I was a girl I was fascinated by the story of the maiden and the water horse, so it has stuck in my mind."

"I'd like to hear it," Nate said. He couldn't sleep anyway.

"Long ago my people used to camp by the lake every summer. One year they went and discovered the Utes on the other side. The Utes were our enemies then, so there were a few clashes but no lives were lost. Well, one morning a Shoshone maiden was out picking berries. An Ute warrior who had been sent to spy on our village spotted her and fell in love with her at first sight. He showed himself, and she was as attracted to him as he had been to her. They spent the whole day together, and when they parted, they pledged their undying love."

"Where does the water horse fit in?"

"I am getting to that. You see, the maiden was the daughter of the Shoshone chief, and the young warrior was the son of the Ute leader. That night both tribes held councils and decided to go to war the next morning. The maiden and the young warrior, though, wanted no part of it. They had arranged to signal each other if open hostilities broke out, and they would slip off together."

"This is sounding more like one of those romantic tales Shoshone women love to share."

"Patience, husband. Patience. Late that night the warrior lit a small fire near the lake to signal his beloved. On the other side, the maiden did the same. Each of them took a canoe and rowed toward the middle. But they had only gone halfway when the sky was lit by a falling fireball. It turned night into day. My people and the Utes saw the two lovers and rushed to the edge of the lake."

"Stop right there. First a water horse, now a fireball?

82

Why can't the Shoshones have simple legends like everyone else?"

"Do you want to hear the rest or not?"

"Go on."

"My people and the Utes yelled for the maiden and the young warrior to turn back, but neither would listen. They paddled to the middle, and the maiden climbed into the warrior's canoe. Everyone saw them embrace. And everyone saw the water horse rear out of the lake, capsize their canoe, and devour them."

"Are there any Shoshone legends that have a *happy* ending?"

Winona gouged a finger into his ribs. "Poke fun all you want. I think it is very romantic. They met, they fell in love, they died in each other's arms. What could be better?"

"Living to a ripe old age?"

"If you really wanted to, you would not be going to Bear Canyon. At least we will be together. If I must die, I want it to be at your side."

Winona closed her eyes and nuzzled against him, leaving Nate with considerable to ponder as the quarter moon arced at a snail's pace across the starry sky. Losing Winona would be more than he could endure. He almost regretted agreeing to help Teeth Like A Beaver. Almost.

Sleep was a long time coming. It seemed as if Nate had just closed his eyes when he felt Winona sit up, and he opened his eyes to behold a pink tinge to the east. In another half an hour the sun would rise. "Good morning, beautiful."

"What would you like for breakfast? We have plenty of flour left."

"Just coffee."

"That is all?"

"A full stomach makes a man sluggish," Nate commented. And he needed to be fully alert and sharp when they reached their destination.

The warriors were also rising. Not one looked as if they had enjoyed a good night's sleep. Like Nate, they had no appetite.

Only Evelyn was bright-eyed and cheerful. She bounced out from under her blankets, raring to go. Winona fed her pemmican and a roll saved from the day before, and within twenty minutes they were mounted and filing over the bluff.

The lowland was as arid as it was dead. A few hardy scrub bushes were all that grew. Nate saw only one living thing, a large brown moth fluttering off to wherever it holed up during the day.

Boulders were everywhere, some the size of a chair, some higher than Nate on horseback. Here and there were rocky knolls and an occasional hill. Other than the sigh of the wind and the thud of hooves, a nigh-complete stillness prevailed.

Teeth Like A Beaver took the lead again. On the lookout for more landmarks, he was constantly rising up off his sorrel to scan the countryside. "We should see it soon," he said after the tenth or eleventh time.

"See what?" Nate asked.

"A hill with a flat top. It is a sign we are near the canyon."

No sooner were the words out of the old Shoshone's mouth than a hill appeared to the northwest. Instead of a rounded summit, it was as flat as a flapjack, as if the crest had been sheared off by a giant's oversized blade.

"There!" Teeth Like A Beaver exclaimed. "Soon, now! Very soon!"

Nate glanced back down the line. No one seemed particularly overjoyed at the prospect. Only Hunts Elk and Rabbit Tail had arrows nocked to their bows, while Man Without A Wife and Humpy were holding their lances close to their shoulders, girded to throw or thrust as the need warranted.

Beyond the flat hill a plateau materialized, an unusual

plateau in that its sides were solid rock hundreds of feet high. Teeth Like A Beaver studied it, then reined to the right, slanting toward the center. "We must look for a crack," he said.

Nate surveyed the plateau from end to end but saw no trace of one. He did, however, catch sight of a flock of small birds winging toward the plateau from the east. As they were the first sign of life he had beheld in hours, he marked their flight, curious where they were bound. He saw them gain altitude and assumed it was so they could clear the plateau. But as they started to fly over it, they unexpectedly swooped low and disappeared. He wondered what was up there that would interest them. "Have you ever been to the top?" he asked the old Shoshone.

"No. The inner walls are as shear as the outer ones. To try to scale them is to court death."

"So you have no idea whether there is any vegetation up there?"

"No. Why do you ask?"

Suddenly Winona extended a finger. "Is that the crack you were talking about, Teeth Like A Beaver?"

Nate had to squint against the harsh glare of the sun to see it, a thin black line that curled downward from the summit. What significance it had remained to be seen.

The white-haired warrior chortled. Jabbing his moccasins into the sorrel, he broke into a gallop. "Hurry, everyone! Hurry!" he bawled. "We are here at last! Soon you will see Bear Canyon for yourselves!"

Chapter Seven

"Wait for us!" Nate hollered, but it was doubtful the old warrior heard him. Teeth Like A Beaver was yipping and whooping loud enough to raise the dead. Nate spurred the big stallion forward, the ground inclining by gradual degrees toward a low bench that paralleled the plateau.

When Teeth Like A Beaver reached it, his sorrel slipped and foundered on loose dirt and gravel that covered the slope. Dust and stone cascaded from under its hooves as he hauled on the reins and pumped his legs, goading it higher. "Hurry!" he shouted again, and disappeared on over the rim.

Nate was not about to do any such thing. A misstep would reap disaster should one of their mounts break a leg. Taking hold of the reins to Evelyn's dun, he climbed slowly. Winona led the pack horse.

Nate had no inkling of what to expect once they reached the top, but it wasn't to find a strip of vegetation in the narrow space between the bench and the plateau, an oasis as it were, in the midst of the wasteland. The stallion and the dun suddenly nickered and wanted to go faster, but Nate held them to a safe walk while descending.

"There's a spring, Pa!" Evelyn exclaimed, which explained why the horses were so agitated.

Trees shaded a large pool ringed by sparse grass. Nate drew rein beside it and slid from the saddle. The sorrel was a few yards away, drinking thirstily, but Teeth Like A Beaver was nowhere to be seen. Gazing toward the base of the plateau, Nate saw the old warrior frantically dashing back and forth and running his hands over the stone surface.

"It cannot be! It cannot be!"

"What is wrong?" Nate called, hurrying to investigate.

"The entrance to Bear Canyon is gone!"

"Gone?"

"It should be right here! An opening not much wider than you are tall. But I can not find it. The rock is unbroken."

Stopping, Nate craned his neck back. The plateau seemed to stretch clear to the clouds. He spotted the crack, which was much wider than it had appeared from a distance. It curved toward the bottom in wide, uneven loops, the result, he reckoned, of an earthquake ages ago. It angled to the right about sixty feet overhead so he moved in the same direction and came to the opening Teeth Like A Beaver was so desperately seeking. The rock had shifted in such a way that the right-hand side overlapped the left, effectively hiding the cleft unless one was right in front of it. "Over here," he yelled.

Teeth Like A Beaver came on the run and commenced laughing and giggling as if he had just consumed loco weed. "This is it! This is it! We have done it, Grizzly Killer! At the other end of this passage is Bear Canyon!"

Nate stepped into the opening and felt a dank, cool breeze fan his cheeks. Sunlight penetrated only a dozen feet or so. Farther on, the passage was as dark as a pit, so dark a man wouldn't be able to see his hand in front of his face.

"What are we waiting for?" Teeth Like A Beaver said, and tried to slip past.

"Hold your horses," Nate said, snagging the oldster's arm. "When we go, all of us will go together. There are some things I must do first."

"What things?"

For starters, Nate scouted the belt of vegetation, ensuring it didn't harbor wild beasts or anything else that might harm his daughter. He found rabbit tracks and those of a wandering turtle but no predator prints. Afterward, while he took the packs off the pack animal and piled them near the spring, Winona and Humpy gathered enough firewood to last several days. Man Without A Wife took care of tethering the dun and the youth's mount, and offered to do the same with the pack horse when Nate was done.

All the while, Teeth Like A Beaver paced and muttered and mumbled, anxious to be on their way. He was like a man obsessed. When Only Hunts Elk asked him to calm down, the old warrior did not seem to hear.

"I have never seen my father like this," Only Hunts Elk mentioned to Nate a couple of minutes later as Nate checked the black stallion's cinch.

"Keep an eye on him in the canyon," Nate advised. "We don't want him running off on us."

Only Hunts Elk looked toward the cleft. "Now that I am here, I wish we had not come. Six of us will ride in, but who can say how many will ride back out?"

"Your father made it out. So did Yellow Hand, the old man who told him about this place. We can, too, if we use our heads."

Only Hunts Elk grinned crookedly. "I admire a man with confidence."

The time arrived. Nate watched his wife and daughter

embrace, then he hunkered and Evelyn stepped into his arms.

"You be real careful, Pa. I don't want anything to happen to you."

"Makes two of us." Nate kissed her on the forehead and held her at arm's length. "Stay close to the spring, you hear? Don't stray off."

"You know me, Pa."

"That's why I said it," Nate responded, rising.

Rabbit Tail was bidding his father and uncles good-bye.

"Make a small fire at night, not a large one, so it cannot be seen from far off," Only Hunts Elk instructed his son. "Always keep one eye on the horses. Often they smell or hear things long before we do."

"I will not let you down," Rabbit Tail promised.

Only Hunts Elk wasn't done. "If you see riders coming, hide." He pointed toward the north end of the plateau where part of the rock cliff had crumbled, heaping the earth high with jagged chunks of stone. "There is a good spot."

"We will lie low if anyone comes."

"One last thing, my son. Your grandfather says none of the creatures in Bear Canyon can get out. The canyon walls are too high. But there might be another opening we are not aware of. So—"

"You need not worry, father," Rabbit Tail said a trifle indignantly. "I am old enough to take care of myself. And I will not let any harm come to the girl."

Nate recalled a comment the old warrior had made. "Listen for sounds from above," he interjected. "Your grandfather also said he saw something with wings one night."

Rabbit Tail surveyed the sky. "I will stay alert, Grizzly Killer. You can rely on me."

It twisted Nate's insides to leave his daughter behind, but he did not let on as he forked leather and wheeled the black stallion. Teeth Like A Beaver was impatiently waiting for them at the cleft. Nate steeled himself to ride off.

"Husband?"

Nate shifted in the saddle. Winona had made no move to mount her mare. "What's wrong?"

"I cannot do it. I can't go off and leave her. The mother in me refuses, although the wife in me desires to be by your side."

"It's all right, Ma," Evelyn said cheerily. "I'll be fine."

Winona stepped to the stallion and grasped Nate's left hand in both of hers. The look she gave him, of commingled love and devotion and regret, tugged at Nate's heartstrings. "Stay," he said.

"I am sorry."

"There's nothing to apologize for," Nate said, and bent to kiss her. "Wherever I go, you are always with me," he whispered. "In here." And he touched his chest above his heart.

Winona's eyes moistened. "You are the love of my life. If you do not return, I will wait until Evelyn is old enough to fend for herself and throw myself off a cliff."

"You'll do no such thing," Nate said, grinning to make light of it, but he knew as surely as he was sitting there that she would do exactly as she said.

"Grizzly Killer! We waste daylight!" Teeth Like A Beaver complained.

Straightening, Nate caressed Winona's chin, shot a last glance at Evelyn, and trotted to the opening.

The old warrior was fidgeting as if ants swarmed in his leggings. "I will lead the way. Keep your head down. The roof is high in some spots, low in others." Teeth Like A Beaver prodded the sorrel into the gap but the horse balked at the close confines. He had to force it to go on.

Nate followed, the passage barely wide enough for the stallion to get through. A dozen steps in, it bore sharply to the left. Inky blackness enveloped them. Total, complete darkness. The stallion snorted but kept walking, the clomp of its hooves pealing loudly on the stone. Heeding the oldster's warning, Nate leaned over the saddle horn.

"I do not like this," Only Hunts Elk commented. "I must have been crazy to allow my father to bring us."

Teeth Like a Beaver heard him, "You never did like closed-in spaces, son. Be strong. It will not last long."

Nate didn't like being hemmed in, either. If the ground were to shake, the walls would close in, crushing them to a pulp. He strained his eyes for a hint of daylight, to no avail. The passage wound on and on. When someone commenced humming, he thought his ears were playing tricks on him.

"Is that you, father?" Only Hunts Elk called out.

"Yes," Teeth Like A Beaver answered.

"What do you have to hum about?"

The elder Shoshone's answer echoed hollowly. "I am happy, my son. Happier than I have been in many winters. Soon I will be reunited with Bright Morning in the other world. I can hardly wait."

Nate had never met anyone so eager to die in all his born days. Without warning his right ankle scraped against the wall, and he winced. Reaching out, he established that the passage had narrowed slightly.

The stallion rounded a corner. How it knew the turn was there was beyond Nate. He couldn't see his hand when he held it in front of his face.

Another bend had to be negotiated. And another. Nate felt a vagrant breeze, or the suggestion of one. Hopeful they were nearing the end, he sat up, and immediately regretted it when the roof gouged his forehead. Snatching his beaver hat before it could fall, he bent back down, his chest against the stallion's neck.

"I see sunlight!" Teeth Like A Beaver exclaimed.

Nate didn't, not until the stallion clomped around a fourth turn. Ahead, a tiny square of light gleamed like a lighthouse beacon. Nate had to suppress an impulse to bring the big horse to a trot. He didn't care what awaited them in the canyon; he just wanted out of there.

The light was blotted out, and for a pulse-racing moment Nate thought he had somehow taken a wrong turn. But no, the sorrel and the old warrior were to blame. A few more yards and Nate could see them, outlined by the opening.

Every nerve aflame, Nate gripped the Hawken in both hands. It wouldn't be long now. He was about to behold what no other white man ever had. He was about to step from the present into the past.

The light expanded. Teeth Like A Beaver laughed and slapped the sorrel.

"Wait for us!" Nate hollered, but he might as well have saved his breath. The old warrior melted into the bright haze. An outcry sounded, and a whinny.

Fearing calamity, Nate slapped his reins against the stallion and sped out of the passage. Brilliant sunlight assaulted his senses. Coming so soon after the complete darkness, it was like having a lit torch thrust into his face. He reined up, the world a blur, disoriented and dreading he had blundered as badly as the Shoshone.

Blinking to clear his vision, Nate heard Teeth Like A Beaver say, "It is just as I remembered, Grizzly Killer!"

Their surroundings snapped into focus. To Nate's left was the white-haired warrior, gaping at what lay below. The passage had opened out on a rise, affording them an unobstructed view of the grandfather of all bears's domain.

High stone ramparts rimmed both sides, ramparts that caught the sun but did not reflect it to any great degree. Only the top of the walls and the rise were bathed in a golden glow. All else was mired in gloom, in a perpetual gray twilight. Thick, oppressive forest covered every inch of slope between the rock walls and the canyon floor, forest as tangled as a briar thicket, the trees bent and misshapen as if deformed by the lack of sunlight. Vines and creepers interwove with grotesquely contorted branches, while moss clung to the trunks and carpeted much of the ground underneath.

It was a forest unlike any Nate had ever beheld, the forces of creation gone amok. Peering into the woodland's murky depths, Nate had no difficulty envisioning all manner of bestial inhabitants, four-legged and two.

At the bottom flowed a stream, but no ordinary waterway. Its waters were as black as the passage, with nary a ripple to disturb its Stygian surface, a clue it might be ungodly deep and hellishly swift.

Bordering the stream were blocks and pieces of rock in all shapes and sizes. Scattered among the trees were others, leading Nate to the conclusion that Bear Canyon was actually the *inside* of the plateau. Long ago, a geologic upheaval of cataclysmic proportions had caused the plateau to buckle and collapse, creating a pocket world isolated by the high outer walls, which were largely intact. For eons it had been a dominion unto itself, a lost land known only to those who were unfortunate enough to stumble on the secret entrance.

Of course, none of Nate's speculation explained where the creatures rumored to exist in the canyon came from. His best guess was that once a larger opening to the outside world had existed, an opening long since closed.

Some mysteries would always remain mysteries.

Gazing out over the misshapen forest, Nate was gripped by a peculiar unease, a feeling of being in the wrong place at the wrong time. Or, more precisely, of being displaced in time, of having broken the boundaries of what was and ventured into a flourishing pocket of what had once been.

"Apo, preserve us!"

Only Hunts Elk, Man Without A Wife, and Humpy were gawking at the same sight in undisguised dismay.

"We should not have come," Man Without A Wife declared. "We do not fit here."

Teeth Like A Beaver dismissed the idea with a curt wave. "You talk nonsense. Bear Canyon is no different than any other except it is the home of creatures that should have died out when our ancestors were young."

The creatures. Nate scanned the forest but saw nothing. Only then did the uncanny silence register. He couldn't hear a single, solitary sound.

"Where is the shelf you have come so far to find, father?" Only Hunts Elk asked.

"The shelf?" Teeth Like A Beaver repeated and swiveled to the north. "It should be right about there." He pointed at a spot a quarter of a mile distant, midway between the canyon floor and the ramparts.

All Nate saw were more impenetrable trees and undergrowth, forming an unbroken canopy. "Could you be mistaken?"

"No, that is where the shelf was," Teeth Like A Beaver insisted. "I am sure of it. But seventy winters have gone by. The vegetation is higher on the slopes than it once was. It has overgrown the shelf."

Man Without A Wife kneed his mount closer to the sorrel. "How do you expect us to find it in *that?*"

"All we have to do is locate a flat spot and dig. When we strike gravel, we will have found the shelf."

"And what will we dig with?" Man Without A Wife asked sarcastically. "Our hands?"

Nate had a more crucial concern. "Forget the shelf for now. We should give some thought to where we want to camp. It will get dark here a lot sooner than it does outside the walls."

"I do not want to camp in the trees," Humpy flatly stated. "Something could sneak up on us and we would never know until it was too late."

"I say we go back out and spend the night with Rabbit Tail and the others," Man Without A Wife suggested.

"Why not just camp here?" Only Hunts Elk said.

It made sense to Nate. They were on the highest point of ground in the canyon. Nothing could get at them without climbing an open slope. "Here is where it will be. But first we must gather firewood and a lot of logs."

"Logs?" Humpy was puzzled.

"We do not have the time to build a lodge so we will build the next best thing," Nate said, heading down. What they needed was a barrier, a breastwork sturdy enough to keep wild animals at bay.

The Shoshones trailed along, Teeth Like A Beaver in a funk because of the delay, the rest glancing nervously about.

The slope was so steep, Nate had to lean back in the saddle, his feet braced against the stirrups, to keep from sliding off. He held the Hawken with one hand instead of two, and prayed they weren't attacked before they reached more level ground. Otherwise, they would be hard-pressed to defend themselves.

Entering the primeval woodland was akin to entering a dream made real. The trees were contorted into grotesque mockeries, their trunks and branches dotted with knobby growths as if something inside sought to burst out. The amount of moss was also alien; many boles were covered from bottom to top. And it wasn't ordinary, moss, either, but a bristly, greenish-red variety, yet another violation of Nature in a canyon rife with them.

The total silence and oppressive gloom produced a sense of foreboding. Nate found himself longing for the sight of a simple sparrow or butterfly. But the only living thing he spied was a sluglike creature crawling along a limb, a greenish thing with two long antennae and purple dots where eyes should be. Involuntarily, Nate shuddered.

"This is an evil place," Only Hunts Elk expressed the sentiments of all of them.

"I told you we should not have come," Man Without A Wife said. "Father and his ridiculous request!"

Teeth Like A Beaver resented the slur. "Leave if you are afraid. All of you! I can do what needs to be done alone."

"We will not abandon you, father," Humpy said. "If

Grizzly Killer is willing to stick by your side, can we, your own flesh and blood, do less?"

Unknown to Humpy, Nate was having second thoughts. He had a powerful hankering to light a shuck, but he had given his word and he would abide by it, come what may. "Humpy, I want you and your father to stay close to the rise. Gather enough firewood to last us the night."

"What about the rest of you?"

"Only Hunts Elk and Man Without A Wife are coming with me to hunt for logs," Nate said, winding lower. Minutes elapsed, and they failed to spot any.

Then, as Nate was skirting heavy undergrowth, Only Hunts Elk said his name. Glancing back, Nate saw the two warriors gazing at a nearby tree in wonderment and not a little apprehension.

Twenty feet up were dozens of teeth and claw marks. Black bears and grizzlies routinely marked trees, but Nate had never seen slashes as deep or as high as these. Whatever made them had stood twice as high as a grizzly and had a much greater reach.

"The grandfather of all bears," Only Hunts Elk breathed in awe. "It is not dead, after all. It must live forever, as the legends claim."

Nate preferred a more logical explanation. "Or else there is more than one, and they have been breeding down through the years."

"Those marks are recent," Man Without A Wife noted. "Made in the last seven or eight sleeps."

Or less, Nate mused, surveying the shadowed landscape. What if, he asked himself, the thing was out there right that second, watching them? He shook his head to dispel the troublesome thought and kneed the stallion on.

There had to be some logs, Nate reasoned. Trees were forever falling, either from disease or strong winds or old age. In a forest that size, there should be scores. But five more minutes of riding yielded none.

"Perhaps we should try down near the stream," Man Without A Wife suggested.

Nate would rather they didn't. Dragging enough logs to the rise would take until midnight, and they needed to be done by dark. Before he could bring it up, however, he rode around a bush bearing thorns as long as his little finger and set eyes on a spectacle that caused him to rein up sharply in amazement.

Trees lay sprawled in a straight line for hundreds of feet. They had been forcefully uprooted and knocked over by something immense, something that had barreled through them like a bull through wheat. Whatever it was, the thing had shattered trunks like kindling and left scores of branches strewn about.

Huge tracks demonstrated a living creature was to blame, and not a freak tantrum of the elements.

Only Hunts Elk was stunned. "What could have done this, Grizzly Killer?"

"Surely not a bear," Man Without A Wife said.

Dismounting, Nate sank onto a knee. He knew every type of track made by every animal in the mountains but he had never seen any remotely resembling the bizarre footprint in front of him. It was three times the length of his own, and half again as wide. Shaped a lot like a sickle, the sole curved in an arch from the toes to the heel. Long indentations at the ends of the four stubby toes could only have been made by claws. But what claws! Each was as long as Nate's hand, and curved like the sole.

Man Without A Wife brought his mount up next to it, stared a moment, and stated, "We are all going to die."

"I would like to see what the animal looks like," Only Hunts Elk said. "We should follow the spoor."

Man Without A Wife snickered. "Did a rock drop on your head when no one was looking, brother? Whatever did this"—he nodded at the path of unbridled destruction—"would tear us to pieces without trying."

"We are *not* going to track it." Nate nipped their disagreement in the bud. He indicated the sun, which had passed its apex and was on its westward descent. "Unless you want to sleep in the open tonight, unprotected?"

"That would not be wise," Man Without A Wife admitted.

Nate took his rope off his saddle. "Give me a hand." Thanks to the juggernaut responsible for the devastation, they now had more than enough logs to suit his purpose. "We have work to do."

The remainder of the afternoon was spent hauling logs to the cleft. It was hard, grueling work. Each tree had to be trimmed and cropped. Then the rope was tied fast and a horse dragged the tree off. Nate rotated the animals so as not to unduly exhaust them.

Once enough had been collected, the logs were arranged in a shoulder-high inverted V, the open part toward the cleft, the point toward the deep woods. By chopping notches in the ends and interlocking them, one on top of the next, Nate constructed a sturdy barrier. Nothing could get at him and his friends without coming over it—or crashing through.

Humpy helped out once he was done gathering firewood. Teeth Like A Beaver, however, sat and stared glumly at where he believed the shelf to be. Every now and then he would say almost tenderly, "Tomorrow, my love. Tomorrow."

Just as the last vestige of sunlight faded, they finished. Nate guided the stallion and the sorrel through a narrow gap between the open end of the V and the high stone wall.

At that juncture, from the inky bowels of the canyon, came a ferocious roar.

"It has begun," Teeth Like A Beaver said.

Chapter Eight

Pilgrims new to the Rocky Mountains often wondered why they saw so few bears, mountain lions, and wolves when the mountains were supposed to be teeming with them. The newcomers didn't realize that during the day, when people were most active, the majority of predators were resting up in their dens.

Only after the sun sank did meat-eaters go on the prowl. Nighttime was *their* time, a time to hunt, to stalk unwary prey, to fill an empty belly. Fang and claw ruled the darkness. It was the survival of the fiercest, and in the grand scheme of things, man's ferocity ranked as low on the scale as a chipmunk's.

Bear Canyon had a reputation for being home to creature the likes of which few had ever seen and fewer still would ever want to. Once the sun set, it lived up to its legend. The formerly silent forest resounded to a savage cacophony of hideous cries, as if the gates of Hell had spilled open and unleashed a legion of the damned.

David Thompson

There were roars, snarls, and snorts. There were screams, screeches, and ungodly wails. From all quarters the sounds issued, an unending chorus of beastly bedlam that echoed and reechoed off the high canyon walls.

Nate had never heard the like. It wasn't that there were so *many* feral cries. It was that so many were so different from those he was accustomed to. Roars louder than any grizzly's could ever be. Growls that rumbled like thunder. Screams so shrill, Nate would swear they were human in origin. And there were other noises, fearsome yowls and ghastly ululations that grated on the nerves and turned a man's blood to ice.

As a precaution, Nate hobbled the horses so they wouldn't run off. They were prancing and nickering in a perpetual fright, the sorrel the most agitated of all.

The Shoshones lined the breastwork, their faces unnaturally pale. Not one spoke, including Teeth Like A Beaver, who had been there before and had some inkling of what to expect.

Nate didn't blame them. Their voices might attract the interest of one of the monstrosities below. It was why they had gone without a fire and partaken of pemmican and jerky instead.

A booming roar broke out at the base of the grassy slope, a roar so loud, the short hairs at the nape of Nate's neck prickled. He heard the crash and crackle of limbs, then a high-pitched squeal and violent thrashing. A predator had found prey.

Nate wished he could see what they were, but he wasn't about to try and satisfy his curiosity. It didn't help that the canyon was as pitch black as the cleft. Only a few stars were visible. The moon had to be up, but until it cleared the east rim, he and the warriors might as well be wearing blindfolds.

"Do you hear that?" Humpy suddenly whispered.

Nate cocked his head. It took a few moments for a

distinct *crunch-crunch-crunch* to register, the grinding of teeth on bone.

"What *is* it?" Humpy breathed in unconcealed terror.

His query was punctuated by the sorrel, which whinnied loudly. The crunching immediately ceased. Underbrush crackled as the creature came nearer.

"We have to keep the horses quiet!" Nate directed. "Another whinny and that thing will be up here after us." He dashed to their mounts. Seizing hold of the stallion, he folded his hand around its muzzle.

Only Hunts Elk, Man Without A Wife, and Humpy had leaped to comply, each taking hold of their own animal.

Teeth Like A Beaver, however, hadn't moved. He was standing near the point of the V, gazing wistfully at the heavens, lost in bittersweet memories.

"Father!" Only Hunts Elk said. "Your horse!"

The old warrior gestured as if to say he couldn't be bothered.

Nate saw the sorrel bob its head. He sprang, hoping to forestall yet another nicker, but he was a fraction too late. The sound carried down the slope to the ebony wall of vegetation and was answered by an ominous snarl.

"It's coming!" Humpy exclaimed.

That it was. Branches cracked like gunshots. Massive paws thumped the earth. The tall grass rustled as a gigantic shape loped toward the breastwork.

Nate heard raspy wheezing, the laboring of oversized lungs. An enormous shape loomed ever larger.

"Father!" Only Hunts Elk whispered.

As calm as could be, Teeth Like A Beaver faced the hulking behemoth.

Although Nate couldn't be certain, it appeared as if the old man smiled. They were forgetting Teeth Like A Beaver *wanted* to die, that if he were slain by the grandfather of all bears, he would consider it fitting.

But was the thing that now reared above the breastwork a bear—or something else? As it stood there breathing like a bellows, the quarter-moon rose past the east rim and moonlight flooded the canyon. In the preternatural glow a hairy, hunched form with a head more wolfish than bruin was revealed. Raising its nostrils into the wind, it sniffed several times, then made as if to push on through the barrier.

Fortunately for Nate, the horses were too paralyzed to make any noise. The sorrel was riveted, trembling in its tracks.

The logs withstood the creature. Snarling, it tried again, driving its shoulders into them. The entire wall shifted but didn't collapse. Frustrated, the abomination stepped back and howled.

Nate figured the thing was going to attack. Wedging the Hawken to his right shoulder, he aimed as best he was able at the center of its skull. The ball would probably have no more effect than a pea shooter would on a buffalo, but Nate was not one of those to go meekly to his end. It was not in his nature. He would resist tooth and nail so long as breath remained in his body.

The colossus lifted a massive paw to smash the logs to bits.

At that instant, overhead, a loud beating as of gigantic wings erupted. Wings like those Teeth Like A Beaver once described, wings of an airborne creature that had to be almost as large as the wolfish horror.

Nate was stupefied when the latter whirled and sped down the slope, exhibiting remarkable speed, given its size. With a shattering shriek and in a streak of motion, the winged monster plummeted. A titanic commotion ensued, roars and shrieks that shook the ramparts.

Rushing to the breastwork, Nate spied two forms locked in titanic struggle. Tremendous wings fanned the air. Talons and claws strove for mastery. For minutes the battle waged, until the wolfish creature broke and fled into the forest. The other rose slowly into the sky, and spreading its wings, it banked and glided toward the opposite side of the canyon.

"Is it gone, you think?" Only Hunts Elk breathlessly asked at Nate's elbow.

"For now. But it might come back." Nate had another, more disturbing thought. What if it could fly *over* the walls? His wife and daughter would be in dire peril. He recalled another legend, common to various tribes, about giant birds that once ruled the skies. Thunderbirds, the Indians called them, birds so immense they carried off grown buffalo. "I think we should go back out."

"To the spring?"

"It is safer there." And Nate would be on hand to protect Winona and Evelyn.

"My father would never agree. And if he will not go, neither will I nor my brothers. You, though, need not remain if you do not want to."

Obligation and love waged war as Nate hastened to the horses. "Move them back against the wall," he urged. Snatching the stallion's reins, he remembered the hobble. It had to be removed first.

The Shoshones rushed over, all except for Teeth Like A Beaver, who stayed by the breastwork.

"What are we to do with him?" Humpy asked in exasperation.

"Tie him up, dig a hole, and drop him in it," was Man Without A Wife's idea.

Humpy pivoted. "Why must you always be so cruel to him? Why do you bicker and insult him all the time?"

"Control your anger, little brother," Only Hunts Elk interceded. "Man Without A Wife fools no one. Who was it who suggested we hold a family council? Who was it who argued we should help father? Ignore him, Humpy. He does not really want to drop father in a hole."

Nate was genuinely surprised. He would never have guessed Man Without A Wife cared that much for Teeth Like A Beaver given how often the pair were at each

103

other's throats. "I will ask your father to sit over here by the wall with us," he volunteered.

Training his eyes on the sky in case the flying fury returned, Nate took a couple of steps, then stopped. High overhead the winged monster had materialized against the backdrop of the quarter-moon. It was rising swiftly toward the canyon rim.

Nate's heart leaped into his throat. If the giant bird made it over the top, Winona, Evelyn and Rabbit Tail might be its next victims. They wouldn't stand a chance. Automatically, Nate brought up the Hawken, but he held his fire. The creature was too high. It would be a waste of lead.

Nate saw mighty wings beating in a frenzy, saw the creature gain more altitude. It was almost to the rim. For long, nerve-wracking moments, the thunderbird hung in midair, almost stationary. Its wings were still flailing, but it couldn't seem to rise any higher. It couldn't quite reach the top. Then, with an angry screech, the bird stopped trying, spread its wings, and glided back down into the canyon.

Nate was at a loss. Maybe the thing was too big and heavy to fly that high. Maybe it was injured. Or maybe wind was a factor. He'd scaled many a mountainous height and encountered gusts strong enough to bowl him over. Regardless, he could breathe easier. His wife and daughter were safe. He walked to where Teeth Like A Beaver was peering over the top log.

"The great wolf did not kill me, Grizzly Killer. It could have. It was looking right at me. It knew I was here."

"Your time had not come," Nate said.

"But I *want* to die. It is why I am here. The wolf should have slain me so my sons and you can get on with your own lives."

"Don't die yet. Without you, we cannot find the shelf where Bright Morning is buried. We might pick the wrong spot."

"I had not thought of that. Tomorrow I will show you. Once I have, any animal that wants to can slay me. I will not resist."

Nate racked his brain for a means to convince the old warrior not to court an attack. "Suppose you are eaten. How will we bury you if there is nothing to bury?"

Teeth Like A Beaver grunted. "I had not thought of that, either. It is awful being old. My mind is not as sharp as it once was." He sighed. "Very well. If my illness does not claim me first, I will settle for taking my own life."

"You do not act that ill," Nate remarked. "Maybe you are not as sick as you think. Maybe you have many winters yet to live."

"Never judge the inside of a person by the outside," Teeth Like A Beaver said. "My body may look fine, but inside the sickness is eating me away. I have spells where I am so weak I can barely lift my arms. Earlier, when you and the others were stacking these logs, I was so dizzy I had to go and sit by myself."

"I thought you were sulking again."

Teeth Like A Beaver grinned. "It is hard to tell the difference." His grin faded and he glanced at his sons. "Friend to friend, Grizzly Killer, I do not have long left. A day or two at the most. Each morning it takes all the energy I have to get up. At night my soul pleads with me to shed this body. Soon I will lie down and never get up again."

"Are you in a lot of pain?"

"At times. It comes and goes. When it is really bad, I become irritable. I snap at others without meaning to."

"Have you told your sons this?"

"No. Why add to their burden? Let them think I am an irritable old fool who does not know any better."

Nate put a hand on the other man's shoulder. "I have misjudged you, Teeth Like A Beaver. I apologize."

"We all make the same mistake. We judge others by our own thoughts, forgetting they have thoughts of their own. It took me many winters to learn no two people think alike."

"I wish—" Nate said, but did not finish. Wishes were the last resort of those unwilling to deal with life on its own terms. Instead of wishing for something to happen, a person should go out and *make* it happen. But there was little he could do for Teeth Like A Beaver. The eating sickness—cancer, the whites called it—had no cure.

"I wish many things," Teeth Like A Beaver said, his wrinkles deepening. "When you reach my age, you will know you have lived a full life if your wishes outnumber your regrets." He smiled wanly. "I was the best husband and father I knew how to be. Maybe I was not always wise and caring, but I tried. When I reach the next world I will hold my head high."

"Come sit with us," Nate requested.

"Are you sure my sons want my company?"

"They love you—" Nate began, and suddenly fell quiet as a new sound wafted down the canyon from the north, a sound that spun him around and brought him to the top of the barrier in the blink of an eye. "Do you hear that?"

Teeth Like A Beaver climbed up beside him. "I hear, Grizzly Killer. But it cannot be! Human beings do not live in Bear Canyon."

The sound proved differently. For from out of the land of the past wafted human voices raised in a droning chant that matched the beat of a single drum. Astoundingly, the raucous roars and wails from the forest faded, as if the creatures had paused to listen.

Only Hunts Elk, Man Without A Wife, and Humpy came on the run, clambering up the logs to hear better.

"Who *are* they?" Humpy marveled.

"Whoever they are, we should try to find them," Only Hunts Elk said. "They might be friendly."

"Or they might be just as vicious as the animals," Man Without A Wife noted. "I say we avoid them."

"Maybe they are cannibals," Humpy commented.

Man Without A Wife looked at him. "The red-headed cannibals of long ago? It could be. The grandfather of all bears has survived. Why not them?"

Teeth Like A Beaver made a statement that shocked them all. "It would explain the warrior who disappeared, the one Yellow Hand thought was taken captive."

"You never mentioned it to me," Nate said.

"Nor us," Man Without A Wife declared.

Teeth Like A Beaver shrugged. "I did not think it was that important."

"Let us decide," Man Without A Wife gruffly responded.

"Yellow Hand told me one of his father's friends went to the stream for water. They heard him shout for help and ran down, but he was gone. They found his bow. They also found a partial print that might have been made by a human foot. A big foot, it was. They searched for other tracks but could not find any."

Man Without A Wife frowned. "The grandfather of all bears. A wolf the size of a buffalo. An eagle as big as the wolf. And now savages who ambush warriors. Is it any wonder I want to go beat my head against a tree for being stupid enough to let you bring us here?"

"It is madness for us to stay," Humpy said. "Father, you expect too much of us."

"I expect nothing," Teeth Like A Beaver said. "This is mine to do, not yours. I have said it before and I will say it again. Go if you want. I will not think less of you."

"But we would think less of ourselves," Only Hunts Elk replied.

"Speak for yourself," Man Without A Wife said.

Nate was concentrating on the chant. It rose and fell like a funeral dirge, the beat of the drum never varying. It wasn't musical or melodious like the chants of the Shoshones and other tribes. It was, for lack of a better word, *primitive.* "This changes everything. From here on out, we stick together at all times. No one is to wander off."

The chanting rose in tempo and volume, building to a fever pitch, a lot like the way Shoshones chanted before going on the war path. By now almost all the creatures in the canyon had gone silent.

"Whoever these people are, they have much medicine," Teeth Like A Beaver commented.

"They would need it to live in this terrible place," Man Without A Wife said.

"It is as if the animals are afraid of them," Only Hunts Elk observed.

Humpy chuckled. "I cannot see the grandfather of all bears being afraid of anything."

"Strange we have not see any sign of him yet," Only Hunts Elk said. "Perhaps he is dead."

As if to prove him wrong, out of the murky woods at the bottom of the rise burst a roar as loud as a thunderclap, a roar of primal defiance, of raw challenge, a roar that echoed off the walls and rolled down the canyon to temporarily drown out the singsong chant.

Teeth Like A Beaver went as rigid as a ramrod. "That is him! That is the grandfather of all bears!"

Loud crashing in the brush spurred Nate into wrapping an arm around the old warrior's waist and leaping down from the barrier. Carrying Teeth Like A Beaver as he would a sack of flour, he ran toward the horses.

"Let me go, Grizzly Killer!"

"Only if you promise to keep quiet and keep still," Nate said. The other warriors were hurrying to join him.

Again the night wind bore the rasp of labored breathing, and the ponderous tread of an animal that weighed tons. A tread that drew closer and closer.

"I promise," Teeth Like A Beaver said.

Nate released his hold and tucked the Hawken to his shoulder. Beyond the breastwork another mammoth shape had appeared. The silhouette was unmistakable; that of an enormous bear, its profile similar to a grizzly's, including a bulging hump between its front shoulders.

"It is bigger than the wolf!" Humpy whispered.

That it was, by far. The grandfather of all bears was twice again as large. Halting at the breastwork, it raised its nose on high, sniffing loudly.

"It has caught our scent!" Only Hunts Elk said.

A paw rose in the moonlight, a paw of gigantic proportions. It swept down onto the logs, and with a rending crash fully half were shattered.

"It is after us!" Humpy cried. "We are all dead!"

"Not if I can help it, my son," Teeth Like A Beaver said, and before anyone could think to stop him, he darted past Nate and out into the open, within a dozen feet of the gargantuan brute rearing onto its hind legs.

Nate saw the bear and rise and rise and go on rising until it was as high as a tree. Eyes that glinted in the moonlight fixed on the frail figure of the elderly Shoshone, and a paw that could snap logs like toothpicks rose to swat Teeth Like A Beaver like a fly. "Try us instead!" he yelled to distract it.

Teeth Like A Beaver, his wizened face upturned to the lord of the lost land, started to sing his death song.

Inexplicably, the giant paw did not descend. The grandfather of all bears did not move a muscle.

"Father!" Humpy cried. "Back away from it!"

Teeth Like A Beaver ignored him. Chanting louder, he lifted his arms and stamped his moccasins. He was singing, *"It is a good day to die.... Take me to Coyote.... It is a good day to die."*

Nate didn't know what to make of the bear. It stared at the old man as if mesmerized. Then Teeth Like A Beaver stopped, and as if snapping out of a daze, the bear snorted, dropped onto all fours, and smashed into the breastwork like a runaway steam engine. Chips and slivers flew every which way. A piece as big as Nate's fist struck Teeth Like A Beaver on the temple and he staggered.

Humpy bounded forward. "Father!"

A long leap brought the bear to Teeth Like A Beaver.

Oblivious to the menace, the old warrior resumed chanting and stomping. A mouth wide enough to swallow a horse's head whole yawned wide and lowered toward him.

"Look out!" Humpy cried, shoving his father just as the bear bit down. Teeth Like A Beaver was flung to the ground and was spared. Humpy was not so lucky.

Razor teeth as long as spikes sheared into the young Shoshone above the waist, and he was plucked into the air. He had no time to scream, to call out. The grandfather of all bears shook its prey like a cat shaking a mouse. Humpy's legs flopped from side to side as blood rained down, spattering Teeth Like A Beaver. The bear tilted its head, chomped once, and Humpy was gone above the knees.

"Nooooooo!" Man Without A Wife hollered, charging. His lance grasped in both hands, he speared the tip into the bear's foreleg.

A roar rent the night. The bear jerked back, a stain spreading from the wound. Snarling, it raised a paw to strike Man Without A Wife.

Nate fired. He aimed at an eye as big as a saucer, the only vulnerable spot, but the bear moved just as he squeezed the trigger. He missed the eyeball but must have struck close because the bear roared louder than ever, rotated, and lumbered off into the night, leaving through the opening it had made.

Man Without A Wife went after it, pumping his lance and whooping like a man possessed. He would have chased the bear on down the slope had Only Hunts Elk not overtaken him and seized him by the shoulders.

"Enough, brother! Humpy is gone! There is nothing we can do."

Not to be denied, Man Without A Wife shoved Only Hunts Elk, seeking to break free. "Let go of me!" he raged. "We must slay it!"

Nate dashed to Only Hunts Elk's aid. Between them,

they hauled Man Without A Wife away from the logs and over to his father, who had made no attempt to stand and was gazing sorrowfully in the direction the grandfather of all bears had gone.

"This is your fault!" Man Without A Wife railed, thrusting with the blunt end of his lance but not connecting. "Our brother would be alive if not for your stupidity! His death is on your head!"

"I did not want anyone else to die," Teeth Like A Beaver said. In despair, he pressed his hands to his face and wailed, "What have I done?"

"You cannot blame yourself," Only Hunts Elk said.

Man Without A Wife was practically beside him. "Who else should we blame? Who refused to listen to reason? Who brought us here?"

Teeth Like A Beaver doubled over, his arms clasped to his skinny chest, and shook as if with palsy. "Leave! Now! All of you! I want no one else harmed on my account."

"We will go, father!" Man Without A Wife said. "And we will drag you with us!"

Nate felt air fan his face but did not think much of it. He was more concerned with holding onto the hothead. Not that he figured the warrior would do Teeth Like A Beaver any harm. For a Shoshone to strike another Shoshone was virtually unheard of. For a son to strike a father was unthinkable.

Then air fanned Nate again, stronger than before, and he realized it couldn't be the breeze. It came from directly overhead. His gut balling into a knot, he glanced up.

Not thirty feet above them hovered the giant bird.

Chapter Nine

Mighty wings as long as canoes beat the night in powerful rhythm. Steely talons larger than meat hooks were curled to rip and rend. A yard-long beak yawned wide, releasing a hawkish, ear-piercing shriek, and the monarch of the air dived.

"Get to cover!" Nate bawled, shoving Man Without A Wife and Only Hunts Elk. Both tottered, off balance, stupefied by what he had done until they looked up.

Nate, stumbling backward, grabbed for a pistol. In his haste he tripped over his own feet and fell. Fortunately for him, the giant bird swooped toward one of the horses instead. Toward the sorrel. It whinnied and tried to move toward the gap, but hobbled as it was, the best it could do was awkwardly lurch a few feet.

Saber-sharp talons sliced into the sorrel's back. Nate heard flesh rip like cloth, heard the animal's spine crack and saw dark geysers spray from the sorrel's nostrils.

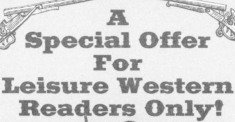

A Special Offer For Leisure Western Readers Only!

Get FOUR FREE* Western Novels

Travel to the Old West in all its glory and drama—without leaving your home!

Plus, you'll save between $3.00 and $6.00 every time you buy!

GET YOUR 4
FREE* BOOKS NOW—
A VALUE BETWEEN
$16 AND $20

Mail the Free* Book Certificate Today!

FREE* BOOKS
CERTIFICATE!

YES! I want to subscribe to the Leisure Western Book Club. Please send me my 4 FREE* BOOKS. Then, each month, I'll receive the four newest Leisure Western Selections to preview FREE* for 10 days. If I decide to keep them, I will pay the Special Member's Only discounted price of just $3.36 each, a total of $13.44 ($14.50 US in Canada). This saves me between $3 and $6 off the bookstore price. There are no shipping, handling or other charges.* There is no minimum number of books I must buy and I may cancel the program at any time. In any case, the 4 FREE* BOOKS are mine to keep—at a value of between $17 and $20!

*In Canada, add $5.00 Canadian shipping and handling per order for first shipment. For all subsequent shipments to Canada the cost of membership in the Book Club is $14.50 US, which includes $7.50 shipping and handling per month. All payments must be made in US currency.

Name _____

Address _____

City_____ State_____ Country_____

Zip_____ Telephone_____

Tear here and mail your FREE book card today!*

Get Four Books Totally
F R E E* –
A Value between
$16 and $20

Tear here and mail your FREE* book card today!

PLEASE RUSH
MY FOUR FREE*
BOOKS TO ME
RIGHT AWAY!

LeisureWestern Book Club
P.O. Box 6613
Edison, NJ 08818-6613

Convulsing wildly, the horse squealed as the giant bird, venting shrieks, rose into the air again.

Neither Only Hunts Elk nor Man Without A Wife attempted to stop it. Riveted, they gaped at the aerial spectacle of a full-grown horse being carried off as effortlessly as if it were a rabbit or squirrel.

Teeth Like A Beaver pushed past them. "No! Not my horse!" He jumped at the sorrel's hind legs but fell short. Spilling onto his knees, he burst into tears.

Nate rose and moved to the old warrior's side. Twenty feet above them the bird of prey climbed rapidly. The sorrel was limp in its grasp, head bowed, legs splayed, either dead or close to it.

"I am sorry," Nate said. "There is nothing we can do."

Man Without A Wife tore his gaze from the feathered devil. "Yes there is! We can leave! Now! Before someone else, or another horse, needlessly dies."

"I will not go unless father does," Only Hunts Elk said.

"What is the matter with you?" Man Without A Wife sniped. "Do you *want* to end up like our brother? Help me throw father onto Humpy's mount."

"No."

Man Without A Wife gave voice to a growl of stifled rage and bafflement. "Do as you want, then! All of you! I have had enough." Stalking to his horse, he removed the hobble and turned toward the cleft. "Last chance. Is anyone coming with me?"

"I cannot," Nate said.

"Fools! You bring your fate down on your own heads. I want no more part of it." So saying, Man Without A Wife tugged on the reins and marched into the opening. Seconds later, out of the passage wavered his spectral voice. "I will wait at the spring with the others. When you come to your senses—if you live long enough—join us. My father's folly is not worth dying over."

"Man Without A Wife!" Only Hunts Elk called, but his

brother didn't answer. "I never thought he would desert us."

And then there were three, Nate thought. And one of them was groveling in misery in the grass. Sliding his hands under Teeth Like A Beaver's arms, Nate boosted him erect. "We cannot stay here. We are too exposed."

"Where would you have us go?" Only Hunts Elk asked. "Down there?" He jerked a thumb at the primeval wilderness.

"No, in there." Nate nodded at the cleft. It would be cramped, and the horses wouldn't be able to lie down, but at least they had a prayer of living out the night. Squatting beside the black stallion, he bent to remove the hobble from around its ankles.

Only Hunts Elk stepped to his bay. "I cannot believe Humpy is gone," he said softly, kneeling. "He was the youngest of my brothers. Although we were winters apart, we were close when we were small. He always looked up to me and did as I did."

"He must have loved your father very much," Nate observed. Only love could compel a man to sacrifice his life as Humpy had done.

"We all do," Only Hunts Elk said, and went on in a whisper. "I do not want Teeth Like A Beaver to know, but the reason we drew sticks was not to pick which of us went after him. It was to decide who had to stay behind. All his sons and grandsons wanted to go, but that was just not practical. Our wives and children needed protecting. A Piegan war party had been seen near our village less than a moon ago."

"Tell your father. Maybe it will change his mind about staying."

"If only that were so. But my father is like a buffalo stampede. He cannot be turned from his path once he has set himself to do something."

"My father was the same way," Nate commented. In a manner of speaking. Nate had many a harsh memory of a hard hickory switch being applied to his backside with all the cruel vigor his father could muster.

Rising, Nate slid the hobble into his saddlebag.

"All the wives my father has had, you would think he had forgotten Bright Morning by now," Only Hunts Elk remarked.

Nate envisioned Winona, and imagined how devastated he would be if he lost her. "Into the cleft. Your father will go ahead of us so he cannot sneak back out in the middle of the night."

They turned toward the old warrior, and froze.

"He is gone!" Only Hunts Elk blurted.

Nate ran to the gap and on out and around to the end of the rise. Halting, he scanned the slope but saw no trace of the old warrior.

Only Hunts Elk was right next to him. "Where can he be?"

Out of the trees came the answer. "Go back, my son. You, too, Grizzly Killer. I do not want anyone else to lose his life on my account."

"Don't do this, father!" Only Hunts Elk cried. "Stay with us until your time has come, as you said you would do."

"Forget about me, son. Go with Man Without A Wife. Grizzly Killer, I release you from your promise. You have done more than I had any right to expect. Now I go to be with Bright Morning, one way or another."

"Father! No!" Only Hunts Elk started down after him.

Nate seized the warrior's wrist. "Use your head," he cautioned. "You will never find him if he does not want to be found."

Only Hunts Elk didn't try to pull away. "You are right," he said. "It would be reckless to go after him."

"Reckless and deadly." Nate let go.

Instantly, the warrior pivoted and sprinted toward the gap. "But I owe it to him and to myself to try!"

"What are you doing?" A hunch galvanized Nate into

115

giving chase. But the stocky Shoshone was fleet of foot and raced behind the barrier well ahead of him. Nate burst on through to find Only Hunts Elk already on the bay and goading it toward the wide opening made by the grandfather of all bears. "Stop! Please!"

Only Hunts Elk smiled, and then was gone. The bay cleared the shattered logs in a splendid jump and galloped headlong down the rise toward the forest teeming with ferocious carnivores.

"Stop!" Nate hollered again as he sprinted to the point of the V. He climbed up in time to catch sight of Only Hunts Elk melting into the vegetation. Off to the right something snarled. To the north a brutish cough further emphasized the peril.

"Damn, damn, damn," Nate simmered, appalled at the turn of events. It would be a miracle if father and son lived out the hour. Hopping down, he hurried to the stallion and was about to climb on when doubt assailed him. *What was he doing? What was he trying to prove?* He had done all that was humanly possible to help Teeth Like A Beaver. His obligation was over. Teeth Like A Beaver had said as much. So why should he risk life and limb in a vain attempt to save someone who did not want to be saved? *Remember Winona and Evelyn,* he reminded himself. He had an obligation to them to stay alive, too.

Nate glanced at the gap and his limbs took on a life of their own. Before he knew it, the stallion was out the opening and trotting down the grassy slope.

The forest closed around him. Nate went a dozen yards when, with a start, he realized he hadn't reloaded the Hawken. Reining up, he corrected his oversight. But he didn't dismount. He reloaded right there in the saddle, so if he suddenly had to get out of there, all he had to do was slap his legs and ride like hell.

The chanting to the north had died down and once again the ancient woodland pealed to the cries of a myriad of beasts. A throaty bellow issued from its depths, a scream knifed the night to the left. And now that Nate was among the trees, he heard other, more subtle sounds. A lot of furtive rustling and skittering. As he poured powder down the Hawken, a sibilant hiss arose.

It brought goose bumps to Nate's skin. Compounding his unease were the grotesque trees. Their twisted limbs and warped boles lent them an otherworldly aspect. He would swear they were alive, and that at any moment they would rise up and swarm over him, entangling him in a suffocating grip.

Enough! Nate mentally chided himself. He was behaving like a ten-year-old! He had to rein in his imagination and steady his frayed nerves. Otherwise he would be jumping at shadows.

As if to mock him, the undergrowth swayed to the movement of a darkling shape. Nate saw a bulky body and a horn or tusk that shimmered like ivory. The thing grunted, paying him no mind, which was fine by Nate. Fingers flying, he finished reloading and slid the ramrod back into its housing under the barrel.

Now that he was ready to start searching, Nate was unsure how to go about it. He couldn't just commence shouting for the two warriors. Every predator within earshot would come on the run. Crisscrossing the valley would be equally futile. He was bound to run into another ravening monster long before he stumbled on those he sought.

Now that he thought about it, Nate decided it had been a mistake to leave the relative safety of the rise. Only Hunts Elk would return there eventually, provided he survived. As for Teeth Like A Beaver, there was no telling what he would do.

Or was there? Nate speculated. More than anything else, Teeth Like A Beaver desired to be with Bright Morning. So it made sense the old warrior would head for the shelf where she was buried.

Against his better judgment, Nate wheeled the stallion

and threaded through the thick vegetation. He moved at a slow walk, reining up constantly to listen and look. Twice he saw large animals but neither bothered him. Whether they were meat-eaters or plant-eaters, he couldn't say.

Nate had a general notion of where the shelf lay, but finding it would take some doing without landmarks to go by. The maze of trees and brush compounded his problem. He was forever skirting thickets and other obstacles, which led him father and father astray.

In more than an hour Nate covered only a couple of hundred yards. Presently, he came to a grassy bank. It wasn't steep so he went straight up, and as his head rose above the crest he spotted a clearing ahead. In the center, cloaked in shadow, was a two-legged figure.

Thinking he had found Teeth Like A Beaver, Nate beamed and raised an arm to wave. But something about the figure gave him pause, and he reined up. It was a lot taller and broader than the old Shoshone. Little else was apparent.

Then the figure stepped from the shadows into a shaft of moonlight filtering through the canopy.

Nate didn't move, didn't scarcely breathe.

It was human. Or rather, human*like*. The moonbeam accented its craggy features; a wide nose, thick lips, sunken cheeks and a jutting, bony jaw. It had a thatch of black hair that hung in disheveled strands, framing its beetling brow and bushy eyebrows. Hunched shoulders wider than Nate's bulged with muscle, and thick sinews rippled on its arms and legs. A barrel chest, broad hips, a ragged animal skin around its waist, and a long, stout wooden club in its knobby right hand completed the image.

The next moment, from out of the shadows stepped two more. Physically, they were almost identical. Like the first, their loins were covered by crude hides. One held a bone club, the other a plain spear fashioned by trimming a thick branch and chipping at the end to make a point.

Nate didn't hail them, didn't do anything to give his

presence away. They were men, but they were not men. They radiated an air of sinister savagery, as if all that was brutish and violent and wild in human nature had been clothed in flesh and bone. The Shoshones would call them bad medicine. To Nate, they were predators every bit as dangerous as the grandfather of all bears and the other creatures infesting the canyon.

The first one sniffed the breeze. He appeared to be the leader, for when he abruptly darted toward the side of the clearing and flattened behind a large log, the others followed his example.

Seconds later another shape materialized across from them. But it had four legs and slunk low to the ground in fluid pantherish movements. It was a huge cat, or lion, with a tawny coat dappled with spots and a bobbed tail like that of a bobcat or lynx. Its canine teeth protruded from under its upper lip, each as long as a Bowie.

The cat moved slowly, warily, its head constantly shifting. When it came to the center of the clearing, to where the three beast-men had been standing, it lowered its nose to the earth. A low growl filled the night, and the cat began to back away.

Nate was astounded. The cat was acting spooked, as if it were afraid. Yet that didn't seem likely when it was big enough to bring down a bull buffalo.

Suddenly the beast-men hurtled from concealment. They weren't running *from* the cat; they were sprinting *toward* it in long bounds worthy of antelope. They were on the cat before it could flee, although it tried to by whirling toward the trees.

As the long-tooth turned broadside, the beast-man wielding the thick spear let his weapon fly. The spear was bigger by far than a Shoshone lance; at least eight feet in length and as thick around as Nate's upper arm. It had to be heavy, too, eight or ten pounds, or more, yet the beast-man hurled it with such force the spear cleaved clean through the cat's body, the tip jutting out the other side.

The long-tooth tumbled, then rolled about on the moss, screeching and caterwauling and clawing in vain at the object that had brought it low. In its rage and agony it disregarded the three brutish figures until it was too late.

The first beast-man brought his wooden club crashing down on the long-tooth's skull. Sixty feet away, Nate heard the thud and crunch. The cat collapsed, limp but still alive, as the beast-man with the bone club swung in an overhand arc.

More blows followed, a deluge of clubs and fists and feet. The spear was wrested out and plunged into the cat again and again and again. When the beast-men finally stepped back, the long-tooth was a bloody ruin, torn and ripped and broken. And dead.

The first beast-man threw back his head and roared in triumph. The others joined in, and every last creature within earshot fell silent.

Here were the true lords of the lost canyon. Men as beastly as the beasts themselves. Men strong enough and savage enough to contend with the long-tooths and big bears on their own terms. Men in whom there was no hint of weakness.

Soon the roars ended. The first beast-man bent over the cat, his right hand probing the spear wound. Fingers as thick and blunt as chisels dug into the body. After a bit he pulled his bloody arm out and held it up for the others to see. Clutched in his hand was the long-tooth's heart.

The beast-man took a hungry bite and chewed with relish. After taking another, he passed the heart to a companion, who repeated the ritual and passed it to the third. The remainder was given back to the first beast-man, who held it aloft as if offering it to some primitive god. Then he stuffed the morsel into his mouth.

Nate had witnessed all he cared to. He wanted to get out of there before he was discovered. Lightly handling the reins, he started to turn the black stallion around. The horse made little noise, certainly not enough that any nor-

mal man would hear. But the three beast-men spun and
crouched, their beady dark eyes scouring the woods.

Instinct compelled Nate to spur the stallion into a trot.
He raced into the trees, seeking to put as much distance
as possible between the ogres and himself. But when he
glanced back, the trio were in determined pursuit, bounding after him with startling swiftness.

Nate brought the stallion to a gallop, his forearm in
front of his face to protect his eyes from limbs and brush
that tore and gouged. He was heading west, he thought,
and hoped against hope to come on open ground where
the stallion's speed and stamina would give him an ad-
vantage.

No such luck. The vegetation presented an unbroken
tangle no matter which direction Nate angled. Avoiding a
tight cluster of trees, he ducked under a low limb, weaved
through several boulders, and looked over his shoulder to
see if he had gained any ground. He hadn't. The beast-
men flowed over the moss-covered earth like bloodhounds
on the trail of a coon, the brute with the wooden club in
the lead.

Nate pushed the stallion to its limit. He held his own
until a dense thicket barred his way. To bypass it he
swung to the right, enabling the beast-men to narrow the
distance by cutting through to intercept him. As he flew
around the thicket he heard the slap of naked feet and the
rasp of heavy breaths.

The lead beast-man was almost on top of him. Another
couple of bounds and it would be close enough to use the
club, to bring the stallion down with a blow to the rear
legs.

Shifting in the saddle, Nate extended the Hawken. The
beast-man looked up, into his eyes, and snarled. Nate
curled back the hammer, held the rifle as steady as he
could, and fired just as the creature vaulted forward. He
aimed at the head and the ball struck true, flipping the
beast-man backward.

Facing front, Nate barely avoided a low limb. He wound past a wide trunk and up a small knoll. A glance showed the first beast-man down and the other two standing over him, nudging him with their weapons.

Nate rode on and didn't slacken his pace until the west wall reared high overheard. Drawing rein, he reloaded again, tingling in expectation of being attacked. But the forest in his immediate vicinity was still. He had done it. He had eluded them.

Or so Nate assumed until a keening yowl split the dark and was chorused by others far and wide. He had heard similar cries earlier and mistaken them for the howls of animals. Now he knew different. It was the beast-men, signaling back and forth.

Nate worked faster. When the ramrod scraped the housing, he flinched. In his overwrought state, every furtive sound was made by a slinking beast-man. Every shadow was a beast-man about to spring.

Off toward the stream a new sound swelled, a Shoshone war whoop. Nate paused, listening, positive it was Only Hunts Elk. The whoop was not repeated, and Nate dreaded the worst.

Another keening wail, from high weeds an arrow's flight away, stiffened Nate in alarm. Out of the weeds filed four beast-men, their wide shoulders stooped as they jogged northward. Nate thought for sure they knew where he was, but they vanished into the gloom without once glancing in his direction.

Nate waited a suitable interval, then rode southward. With the woodland swarming with beast-men, his wisest bet was to return to the rise.

Hugging the base of the wall, Nate traveled a hundred feet or so, abruptly halting when what he mistook for a small hill detached itself from the ground and shuffled due east.

The thing had a body shaped like a pine cone and was covered with either scales or armor. It also had a short armored tail tipped by a spiked ball. Of all the creatures Nate had seen so far, it was the most outlandish. He had never heard tell of anything like it.

The creature grunted nonstop, like a hog in a hog pen, its rolling gait reminiscent of a man who had downed too much firewater. Halting, the aberration bobbed up and down.

Nate heard an odd patter, like raindrops, only it wasn't raining. He couldn't imagine what the animal was doing. Then he saw its forelegs were clawing at the ground, that it was digging at a prodigious rate. The patter was dirt being flung in a steady spray.

Nate considered trying to ride on by, but didn't. As enormous as it was, the thing could crush the stallion with a single swipe of its spiked tail. Nate was content to wait while it bored into the earth like a mole gone amok. Its head dipped into the hole, then the front half of its body.

To the northeast a beast-man yowled and was answered by several others off near the stream.

They were still hunting him. Nate scoured the woods, especially his back trail, without spotting any. Through an opening in the canopy he saw something else, though, a flickering pinpoint of light a mile or more away, halfway up the west rampart. It was a fire, and he had a pretty good idea who had built it. The beast-men must have a lair somewhere, and what better place than safely above the canyon floor and the marauding monsters that roamed there?

Nate turned toward the creature with the spiked tail— but it was no longer there. Kneeing the stallion, he passed the huge hole, his finger on the Hawken's trigger. He breathed a lot easier when it was behind him.

More beastly howls sprinkled the canyon, to be eclipsed by the roar of the grandfather of all bears.

Within minutes Nate reached the rise and rode to the top. Entering the breastwork through the gap, he slid down. No one was there to greet him. Humpy's mount was also gone, yet it couldn't have strayed off, hobbled as it was.

Moving to the point of the V, Nate pondered his next step. It rankled him to think his friends were in dire trouble and he was powerless to help. If the beasts didn't get them, the beast-men were bound to.

Adrift in the dark, Only Hunts Elk and Teeth Like A Beaver would be hard pressed to find their way back. Nate weighed the merits of firing shots to attract them. But with the canyon prone to echoes, sounds alone wouldn't suffice. Gazing southward, he glimpsed the pinpoint of light again.

What worked for the beast-men would work for him.

Enough pieces of wood were scattered about for Nate to build a heaping pile just beyond the section of breastwork crushed by the bear. A handful of dry grass served as kindling.

Opening his possibles bag, Nate groped inside and palmed his fire steel and flint. Then, dropping onto his hands and knees, he struck the steel and flint together, showering sparks onto the kindling. Blowing softly, he ignited it, and once small flames were licking the grass, he added larger and larger bits of wood until he had the whole pile ablaze.

Stepping back through the opening, Nate climbed the logs. The fire lit up the rise from end to end. The old warrior and his son were bound to spot it. So would virtually every living creature in the canyon, and some, inevitably, would investigate, but it was a gamble Nate was willing to take. Cradling the Hawken, he mentally crossed his fingers the two Shoshones showed up before anything else did.

Minutes dragged by with no sign of them.

Scanning the tree line for the umpteenth time, Nate saw a lone figure appear. "Teeth Like A Beaver?" he called.

The figure started up the slope toward him. Nate

smiled, only to have his hopes dashed as its hunched form and loping gait became apparent.

Behind it another appeared, and then another.

His gamble had not paid off.

The beast-men had found him first.

Chapter Ten

Nate King had no regrets about the risk he had taken, not when the lives of two fine men were at stake. Besides, it was too late to put out the fire even if he were so inclined. Sighting down the Hawken, he fixed a bead on the chest of the foremost beast-man. When the brute was so close that its beady eyes reflected the firelight, Nate stroked the trigger.

The blast rolled off down Bear Canyon, and the beast-man rolled back down the rise. Its body came to rest at the feet of the other pair, who stopped to examine it.

Their mistake was Nate's salvation. He reloaded, and was ready when they roared in unison and barreled up the slope. A shot from the Hawken dropped one, a shot from a smoothbore pistol felled the other.

Hopping off the breastwork, Nate set to reloading both guns, one eye on the forest. He was about done with the rifle when two more hide-clad towers of muscle bounded into the open and streaked toward the barrier.

Nate aligned the Hawken between a couple of logs. He hadn't had time to reload the pistol, but he had another tucked under his belt. The beast-men would never reach him.

Then several others hurtled from the woods, and more on their heels. Seven, eight, nine, and still they came. More than Nate could bring down before they reached him. More than enough to do to him as they had done to the long-tooth.

Nate glanced at the black stallion, then at the cleft. He had time to escape. But the beast-men might follow him—and Winona and Evelyn were on the other side.

Since there had been no evidence of beast-men at the spring. Nate suspected they were unaware of the passage. Once they found a way through to the outside world, they would roam the Rockies at will, slaying countless Indians and whites alike.

Nate resolved to make a stand, to fight until he couldn't fight anymore, for the sake of both his loved ones and untold scores of potential victims. Aiming at the foremost brutish terror, he fired. The slug cored its cranium, jolting it off its feet, but this time the other beast-men didn't stop to examine their fallen comrade. Howling with bloodlust, they converged on the crest.

Nate yanked his other pistol out, extended it between the logs, and squeezed off a shot that pitched a beast-man onto its craggy face.

All three guns were empty. Nate started to reload the rifle but saw the rest would be on him before he could. Dropping it, he drew his Bowie and his tomahawk and clambered to the top to await the onslaught.

Eleven or twelve were rushing up the slope, braying like a pack of coon hounds. The first two reached the breastwork and sprang upward. Grabbing hold of the top log, they sought to bring their clubs into play.

Nate sliced his tomahawk into the creature on the right, then slashed his Bowie across the throat of the one on the

127

left. The first beast-man toppled but the second clung on, spurting like a fountain, and swung, narrowly missing Nate's head. Twisting, Nate buried the tomahawk in the beast-man's beetling brow.

Arms windmilling, the abomination fell. Nate had to firm his grip on the tomahawk so it wouldn't be wrested from his grasp.

An instant later five beast-men surged to the barrier. Springing upward, they sought to overwhelm him by sheer force of numbers.

Nate blocked a club, ducked under a spear, and sheared the tomahawk into a hairy arm. Cold steel bit deep through flesh and bone. Another beast-man swung, a bone club flashing. Nate tried to dodge, but balanced as precariously as he was, he couldn't move fast enough. The club connected, slamming into his shoulder.

The strength behind the blow was incredible. Nate was knocked from his perch and flung like a rag doll to the ground. He landed with a bone-jarring thud, then scrambled upright as beast-men poured over the logs. One leaped straight at him, a wooden club held overhead to bash out his brains.

Behind Nate, a rifle boomed. The ball caught the creature between the eyes and cartwheeled him backward. A second brute fell to a second shot.

Backpedaling to gain room to maneuver, Nate heard a bow string twang. An arrow blossomed in the chest of a beast-man about to jump down.

Shoshone war whoops rose above the din. Suddenly Man Without A Wife and Rabbit Tail were there, Man Without A Wife thrusting his lance into a wildman's belly, Rabbit Tail notching and loosing shaft after shaft.

They weren't alone. Winona planted herself at Nate's side, a pistol in each hand. She shot a beast-man on the verge of springing, shot another that had vaulted through the opening made by the bear.

It was too much. The creatures were savage, but they

weren't stupid. The remaining beast-men broke and ran.

Man Without A Wife and Rabbit Tail whooped and clapped one another on the shoulder.

Nate couldn't credit his eyes. Facing his wife, he touched her cheek. "You saved my bacon," he said softly in English.

"What were you trying to do? Throw your life away?"

A small hand grasped Nate's wrist and he looked down into the angelic features of his daughter. Wisps of gun-smoke curled from the muzzle of her rifle. "You too, little one? You shouldn't have come."

"If we had not come, you would be dead," Winona said matter-of-factly in her own tongue.

Man Without A Wife turned. "I tried to talk her out of it, Grizzly Killer. But when she heard about Humpy, about the bear and the wolf and the thing in the sky, there was no reasoning with her. She insisted her place was with you."

"As it always is," Winona said, beginning to reload.

Nate knew better than to argue. He reloaded, too, as quickly as he could.

Man Without A Wife was gazing around the rise. "Wait. Where are Teeth Like A Beaver and Only Hunts Elk?"

Briefly, Nate related the sequence of events since Man Without A Wife had left. Both Shoshones were thunder-struck. Man Without A Wife reacted by pounding the breastwork in impotent rage.

Rabbit Tail stepped to the opening and stared down into the canyon. "Where can they be?" he asked in blatant misery.

"As soon as it is light, I am going to go hunt for them," Nate said.

"I will go with you," Man Without A Wife volunteered.

"I, also," Rabbit Tail chimed in.

"We will all go, husband." Winona declared in English.

Over my dead body, Nate thought. Aloud, he said, "You

don't realize what you're saying. You haven't seen what we saw. You have no idea what we're up against." She had something to say but he wasn't done. "They are worse than any grizzly, Winona. The stories weren't exaggerated. The legends are true."

"Be that as it may, what would you have Blue Flower and I do? Wait out by the spring by ourselves?"

"It would be safer there, yes."

"I would rather be with you," Winona said with a finality that implied she would brook no dispute.

Nate gripped her by the shoulders. "Please. Listen to me. If you truly love me, if you truly trust me, you will do as I ask and take Evelyn back out. I have never begged you to do anything in all the years of our marriage, but I am begging you now. Please, *please*, for God's sake do as I ask."

Winona bit her lower lip, a sign of indecision.

"I appreciate your feelings," Nate pressed her. "I understand why you don't want to go. Your devotion does me honor. But if you stay, I will be so fearful for your lives that I will be of no use to anyone. *Please,* Winona."

Her mouth quirked downward. "My spirit is torn. My rightful place is by your side. But you have never begged before. As for trusting you, there is no person I trust more. I have given you my heart, haven't I? So if you say it is necessary, I will go, even though I do not like being separated."

Nate embraced her and kissed her on the neck. "When this is all over," he whispered, "we'll leave Evelyn with Zach and go off by ourselves for a week or two."

"I will hold you to that, husband."

Nate walked her to the cleft, Evelyn's hand in his. As they reluctantly entered, he thought of how scared his daughter would be, wending their way back in the dark, and said, "Hold on." Dashing to the fire, which had burned low, he selected the best brand and gave it to Winona. "So you don't stub your toe."

Evelyn hugged his leg. "Be careful, Pa."

"Always." The stomp of a hoof reminded Nate of another step he should take. He handed the stallion's reins to his wife. "We've already lost two horses," he explained.

Mother and daughter led the horse in.

Nate stared after them until the torchlight faded. He was glad Winona had gone along with his wishes. Now he could focus on the matter at hand.

Turning to the Shoshones, Nate said, "We will keep the fire going all night." Enough wood was scattered about to suffice. Since the beast-men knew they were there, extinguishing it served no useful purpose. And it might help keep the wild animals at bay. "We can take turns standing guard so everyone can catch some sleep," he added.

Man Without A Wife regarded the sinister veil of darkness. "I doubt I will be able to shut my eyes, Grizzly Killer."

"Me, either," Rabbit Tail said. He was standing over a fallen beast-man, riveted in amazement.

That makes three of us, Nate reflected.

After stoking the blaze, they took up posts along the breastwork, Nate in the center, at the point of the V. The woods were exceptionally quiet, which he took as a bad sign, as proof the beast-men were still below. Perhaps gathering strength for another assault.

After an hour or so, though, the roars and screams of the canyon's many monsters were once again mingling in raucous racket. Nate frequently heard the crash of undergrowth and often saw large fierce eyes flare like burning embers, only to fade because the creatures fought shy of the fire.

Along about four in the morning, the uproar dwindled to an occasional cry. By five the canyon was perfectly still. Every last creature, it would seem, had retired to a den or burrow to rest up until twilight, when another orgy of violence and gore would commence.

The sky gradually brightened. Nate stayed put until there was enough light to pick off a target at fifty yards. It surprised him greatly that the beast-men hadn't reappeared. He speculated the guns had something to do with it, although he couldn't quite conceive of the brutes being afraid of anything.

A more logical likelihood, Nate reckoned, was that one of the slain ogres had been a leader. Among many Indian tribes, when a warrior of note or a chief was slain in battle, the rest sometimes construed it as bad medicine and retired from the conflict.

Then again, Nate realized how silly it was to try and think like the beast-men did. They were so different, so primitive, so much more like animals than men, there was no telling what went through their minds. Maybe they were a superstitious lot, and one of their superstitions had been a factor. Nate simply couldn't say.

"Where should we begin our search?" Man Without A Wife asked, bringing an end to the reverie.

"I heard Only Hunts Elk off toward the stream," Nate recollected. It was as good a place as any to start, and he headed out, avoiding the hairy bodies that dotted the slope. As he passed the last one, it stirred, and a forearm slowly rose toward him. Nate leveled the Hawken but didn't shoot.

The beast-man had taken a slug squarely in the chest, in the sternum, and lay in a pool of drying blood. Scarlet stained its torso and upper legs, and pink froth rimmed its mouth. Eyes the color of coal fixed on Nate and the creature uttered guttural grunts.

"Let me finish it off," Man Without A Wife said, hiking his lance.

"Not yet," Nate said. Cautiously, he bent down, studying the beast-man's features. Intelligence glinted in those dark eyes, intelligence and something else. The brute grunted again.

"He sounds like a bear," Rabbit Tail commented.

Nate thought it was more like a wild boar. Then the beast-man grunted a third time, and Nate divined why. "He is trying to tell us something."

"They have their own tongue?" Man Without A Wife sounded doubtful, to put it mildly.

"Maybe they are more like men than we think."

"I respect you, Grizzly Killer. But in this you are mistaken. They know no more of the ways of human beings than a grizzly does. They live to hunt, to kill. They are more like rabid wolves than like us."

The next second, the beast-man heaved upward, his brawny hand streaking toward Nate's waist, toward the tomahawk wedged under Nate's belt. Springing back, Nate heard the twang of a bow string. In less time than it took to blink, Rabbit Tail sent two feathered shafts into the creature's chest.

Exhaling loudly, the beast-man sank back down. Feebly, he plucked at the arrows, then grunted some more, and expired.

"He almost had you," Rabbit Tail said.

Nate had been in no real danger. But he refrained from criticizing the youth, who only had his best interests at heart.

They moved on after Rabbit Tail and his uncle pulled out the arrows and wiped them clean on the grass.

The spongy moss muffled their tread as they worked their way eastward. Nate noted random patches of blood, and spots where the soil had been torn, clawed and gouged by monsters locked in titanic struggles.

Given all the carnage wrought the night before, Nate had anticipated finding the forms of partially devoured prey. But there were none. Not one carcass. Nor were there any bones from old kills, which struck him as a trifle odd. In the mountains he routinely came across bleached

133

skulls and skeletons, usually those of deer and elk but now and then of other animals.

Either prey slain in Bear Canyon was completely devoured, or *something* came along after the fact and disposed of what was left.

A quarter of a mile from the rise Nate came on another wide hole identical to that made by the armored monstrosity. Only in this instance the earth had been pushed outward, into a large mound, as a mole would do when coming to the surface. More strange curved tracks wandered off into the warped trees.

A little farther on, Nate heard loud buzzing, like that of an entire beehive. Advancing through heavy timber, he crouched when the buzzing grew louder and a shadow flitted overhead. Glancing up, he was astounded to discover an insect circling nearby—a hideous fly as big as a grouse.

Rabbit Tail raised his bow, but Nate motioned for him not to use it. The fly posed no immediate threat. Indeed, it soon swooped low and was gone from view. Pushing on, Nate parted tall weeds and saw it again, roosting atop the remains of a dead animal.

Finally they had found one. And what a find! The thing had been enormous, three or four times the bulk of a buffalo, with a shaggy coat to match. Its four tree-trunk legs were largely untouched, but the body had been ripped open and eaten, exposing ribs almost as long as Nate was tall. A squarish head had been bitten into, though not chewed. At the end of broad nostrils were a pair of blunt horns in the shape of a tuning fork.

But what fascinated Nate the most, and filled him with revulsion, were the things swarming about *inside* the carcass. Some were bugs, or at least looked like bugs. The others were more akin to giant maggots, only these had sawtooth pincers and multiple pointed appendages. They were devouring the body at a fantastic rate, some boring into it like termites into wood, only to reappear elsewhere moments later.

Watching them made Nate's skin crawl. At the rate they were feasting, he figured the whole carcass would be gone within the hour. As he looked on, one of the maggotlike creatures slid off and proceeded to bore into the moss. In a second it was gone, the moss closing over it to betray no trace of its passing.

"They live under the ground?" Rabbit Tail said in horror, gingerly lifting his feet as if he expected an unearthly horde to rise up from underneath and consume him.

"We should move on," Man Without A Wife whispered.

Nate concurred. He couldn't stomach much more. Giving the grisly remains a wide berth, he was soon rewarded with a glimpse of water. "We are almost there," he announced.

The stream was as unnerving as everything else about the canyon. Its inky surface was undisturbed by rocks or rapids, the dark water flowing swiftly past with nary a gurgle or splash.

Nate strode to the edge, then just as quickly backed away.

"Did you see something?" Rabbit Tail asked.

"No," Nate admitted. But the water might be home to denizens every whit as formidable as those that roamed the land and soared the sky.

The narrow shore was devoid of moss, and in the soft earth and mud were imprinted countless tracks, some vaguely familiar, others totally foreign.

Roving northward, Nate hiked around a bend. A crescent clearing abutted the stream, and from it jutted a gravel bar. His eyes narrowed at a new type of track; the hoof prints of a horse.

"Only Hunts Elk was here!" Man Without A Wife declared, dropping onto a knee and placing his left hand

135

over one of the tracks. "His war horse made these. I would
recognize them anywhere."

"Father?" Rabbit Tail said, scanning the vicinity.
"Where can he be? What could have happened to him?"

Nate ventured no reply. The youth was upset enough.
Casting about for more prints, he learned that Only Hunts
Elk had paralleled the stream for a considerable distance,
possibly because the going was easier.

Around the next bend was a larger clearing. And it was
here Nate's worst fears were brought to stark life.

"It cannot be!" Rabbit Tail exclaimed.

But it was. His father's mount, or what was left of it,
lay scattered in bits and chunks. Part of the tail was near
the water. Part of a foreleg was yards away. Half the head
was beside a log, the lips pulled back in frozen fear.

Nate leaped to the conclusion a predator was to blame.
The likely candidate was the grandfather of all bears, or
maybe the giant wolf. But when he scoured the ground,
the only tracks he found were the broad prints of beast-
men.

As best Nate could reconstruct the sequence of events,
Only Hunts Elk had been riding along the water's edge
when over a dozen of the vicious brutes jumped him from
ambush. The warrior had resisted but had been over-
powered. Then the creatures had slain his horse by sav-
agely tearing it apart.

Heel marks convinced Nate the beast-men had dragged
Only Hunts Elk off. Mulling the implications, he gazed
up the canyon.

"Do you think my brother is still alive?" Man Without
A Wife wondered.

It was a long shot, but Nate had to concede there was
a chance. "My guess is they've taken him to their lair."

"Do you know where it is?"

"I have an idea," Nate said.

"Then you must lead us there," Rabbit Tail interjected.

"We must save my father or die trying. He would do the same for either of you."

"That he would," Nate allowed. "But the beast-men are many and we are few. To bait them where they live would be asking for trouble."

"If you do not want to do it, tell me where their lair is and I will go alone," Rabbit Tail said.

"I did not say I would not help," Nate responded, bothered the youth thought so poorly of him. "But we must keep our wits about us and do this right."

The beast-men had gone north along the stream, the width of their tracks suggesting a steady lope.

Nate moved rapidly, conscious time was of the essence. They had until sunset to find both Only Hunts Elk and Teeth Like A Beaver and make it back to the rise. Otherwise, the odds of any of them making it out of there alive were slim.

Fluttering in a thicket brought Nate up short, but birds were responsible. Ordinary birds, too, a handful of sparrows chirping and flitting about as sparrows were wont to do. Nate found it reassuring, a dash of normalcy in the midst of madness.

The only other creature they saw was a monumental snake, a serpent forty to fifty feet in length and correspondingly thick. It was coiled on a flat rock across the stream, sunning itself. And digesting its last meal, if an hourglass bulge was any indication.

Nate automatically brought the Hawken to bear but the reptile showed no interest in them. He gathered it was dozing. Still, he treaded lightly until it was no longer in sight.

Another problem arose. Half a mile farther the tracks of the beast-men ended; they had waded into the stream.

Loathe to do the same, Nate opened his possibles bag, brought out the spyglass, and ranged it over the opposite bank. Determining where the beast-men had emerged was ridiculously simple. A well-worn trail led off through the woods.

"What are we waiting for?" Rabbit Tail chafed at the delay.

"The whites have a saying," Nate commented. " 'Fools rush in where wise men fear to tread.' We would do well to remember that."

"All I care about is that my father is missing."

"Practice patience, nephew," Man Without A Wife said. "Grizzly Killer is doing what is best. Trust him."

The forest on the east side was as choked with growth as the forest on their side. Nate lost the trail amid the trees, and although he looked and looked, he couldn't find it again. Then, acting on the assumption the beast-men had been making for higher ground, he trained the spyglass above the tree line.

The trail was there, all right, meandering to the north. In another half a mile it climbed to a barren bench. Since Nate saw no sign of a trail above it, he deduced the lair must be the bench itself. It was midway up the wall, exactly where the pinpoint of light had been. "We have to cross over."

"The current is strong," Man Without A Wife said, pointing, "and I am not much of a swimmer."

Nate had a problem of his own. Wet powder was as useless as teats on a bull. Somehow he must reach the other bank without becoming soaked. A raft would take too long to construct, so he had to improvise. "We need three logs and three long poles."

It took longer than Nate liked. Most logs they found were either covered with a slippery coating of moss or too rotten to be of any use. And finding three poles long enough to suit Nate's purpose was a chore and a half. But at last they were ready. Each of them carefully pushed a log into the water and straddled it.

Close to land the current wasn't strong, but that changed drastically when Nate pushed off. Since he had come up with the brainstorm, he felt obligated to cross first. He poled once, poled twice, and suddenly felt a powerful tug on his moccasins. Before he could brace himself, the log shot toward the middle.

"Grizzly Killer, beware!" Man Without A Wife yelled.

Nate thought the warrior was referring to the current until he looked up. A gigantic dark shape had broken the surface—and was coming directly toward him.

Chapter Eleven

Before straddling the log, Nate had loosened his buckskin shirt and slid the Hawken down his back to free his hands for poling. So now, when he needed the rifle, he couldn't get to it. Even if he could, he would have thought twice about squeezing off a shot so close to the lair. The beast-men were bound to hear and pour down to investigate.

A fin had cleaved the water. The creature was a fish, but what a fish! It was as long as the log, with a head like a battering ram.

For several tense moments Nate thought the thing would slam into him. At the last split second, though, the fish dived and passed under the log. In doing so, the behemoth brushed against the pole, nearly tearing it from his grasp. Once the creature had passed him, it rose and barreled to the south.

Thinking the worst was over, Nate resumed poling. But he had barely gone a yard when the two Shoshones hollered his name and pointed at the spot where the giant fish had appeared.

Something else had broken the surface, something even larger. Nate realized it was *after* the fish, that the fish hadn't been trying to ram him, but to escape.

The second creature was as wide as a wagon and covered with hair. It had a long neck and the head of a seal. Only no seal ever sported five-inch dagger teeth. Hissing horribly, it gave chase, and as fate would have it, Nate was right in its path. The thing hurtled toward him like a runaway steamboat.

Nate jammed the pole into the bottom and levered forward, striving to get out of its way. But the current resisted, hampering his movements, and before he could try again, the creature was on top of him.

Nate swiveled. Suddenly he was eye-to-eye with it. Unblinking orbs locked with his, and its fearsome mouth yawned wide to rip and rend. Nate clawed for his Bowie, but just when it seemed the thing was about to sink its teeth into him, it dived, plunging under the log. Only it misjudged how deep it had to go.

Nate's left foot flared with pain as the creature struck him. The front end of the log rose out of the water, canting at a steep angle, and he had to clutch it to keep from sliding off. Then it dropped down again, nearly spilling him.

The seal never reappeared but a massive wake marked its course downstream.

Holding the pole with both hands, Nate renewed his efforts. There was no telling what else lurked in the watery depths, and his luck might not hold a third time. He was surprised and pleased to find that toward the middle the current slackened a bit. Enough so he was in no danger of being carried far downstream against his will. He ended up reaching shore thirty yards lower than the point at which he started, but that was to be expected.

Slogging onto land, Nate hauled the log out, set down the pole, and pulled the Hawken up out of his shirt.

The Shoshones had already pushed off.

Man Without A Wife looked as nervous as could be, and Nate didn't blame him. For experienced swimmers, braving those dark waters would be intimidating. For someone who wasn't that adept, crossing would take vast courage. Man Without A Wife poled slowly, moving in short, cautious spurts.

Rabbit Tail followed, frowning, no doubt impatient to find his father. When the nearby water frothed and bubbled, he showed no alarm.

Nate wasn't surprised. It was the nature of the young everywhere to think they were invincible; only with age did they discover calamity had no favorites. He watched the bubbles, expecting another creature to appear, but the disturbance faded without sign of the cause.

It took Man Without A Wife twice as long to reach the bank, and when he finally nosed his log onto the muddy spur, his relief was transparent. "I never want to do that again."

"We will have to, uncle, when we cross back over," Rabbit Tail noted, gliding to a stop beside him.

"Do not remind me."

In single file they hiked toward the bench, sticking to thick cover. When they intersected the trail the beast-men used, Nate avoided it. From his previous encounters, it was plain the wildmen had an exceptional sense of smell, and if something came along after them, the creatures would catch its scent.

Reaching the lair took longer than Nate bargained. It was past eleven, by the sun, when they halted at the bottom of the bench and hid in a thicket to take stock. The slope above them was impossibly sheer; the only way to the top was the trail, and Nate still refused to use it. "We have to circle around," he proposed.

"And lose more time?" Rabbit Tail said.

It couldn't be helped. Nate stalked to the left, never taking his eyes off the rim in case any hairy brutes appeared. The beast-men had chosen wisely. The bench was a natural fortification, an ideal spot to defend, and far enough above the canyon floor to discourage the most determined of predators.

Nate hoped to find a break in the slope, maybe a place where erosion had taken a toll, but it was not to be. Reaching the cliff wall, he pondered whether to go back and use the trail anyway.

"What are those, Grizzly Killer?" Rabbit Tail inquired, nodding.

Carved into the solid stone were scores of handholds and footholds, chiseled out of the very rock.

Sliding the Hawken under the back of his shirt, Nate reached up. The holds were spaced farther apart than they would be if men had made them, but not so far that he couldn't use them. He climbed slowly, alert for signs of activity from above.

Nate tried not to dwell on how high the bench was. He avoided glancing down until he was almost to the top. By then they were well above the treetops, and he had a magnificent view of the canyon from end to end. He spied the rise and the breastwork, saw the dozing snake, saw an elklike animal grazing to the southwest, but also he saw no trace of Teeth Like A Beaver.

Availing himself of another handhold, Nate inched high enough to see what was on the bench. He thought there would be dwellings of some kind, crude hide lodges or brush huts. Instead, he discovered a cave, its entrance forty feet wide and twenty feet high, the earth around it tramped bare. Bones were piled in heaps outside, big bones, little bones, legs bones, rib bones, most cracked or split where the beast-men had broken them to get at the soft marrow.

Of the creatures themselves, Nate saw no sign. Deeming it safe, he thrust his right leg out and gained purchase

143

for his foot. Then, drawing both pistols, he side-stepped to the closest pile and hunkered. Man Without A Wife and Rabbit Tail were not long in joining him.

"We must go in there?" the warrior whispered, not exactly elated.

"If that is where they have taken my father, yes," the stripling responded.

"It would be best if only one of us went," Nate said. To justify his decision, he elaborated. "One can move more quietly than three, and can hide more easily."

"Then it should be me," Rabbit Tail said.

Nate rested a hand on the youth's shoulder. "It is your right, yes, but you are too upset to think clearly. Stay here. I will find your father."

"I should go," Man Without A Wife said.

"You are his uncle," Nate responded, which was no argument at all. To nip debate, he rose and wound through the piles until he was near enough to the entrance to see inside. The cave appeared to be empty.

That can't be, Nate told himself. Moving to the left, he leaned against the rock edge and peeked within. Sunlight penetrated only a dozen yards. It revealed charred embers from last night's fire—and that was all.

Crouching, Nate swung into the opening. Immediately, a nauseating stench struck him with the force of a physical blow and he almost gagged, a sickly sour smell like human sweat only a thousand times worse. He tensed, dreading an outcry, a howl, a roar, anything, but the cave was as silent as a tomb. Perplexed, he stayed where he was until his eyes adjusted.

Fifty feet in, the cave branched into two tunnels. Both were as black as pitch. From them wafted the awful odor. The beast-men were in deeper. So was Only Hunts Elk, if he were still alive.

Nate crept to the tunnels and paused. He had an important decision to make: the right fork or the left? Squatting, he ran a hand over the cave floor, trying to tell whether one tunnel had seen more use than the other. But there was no difference.

Every nerve on edge, Nate chose the right fork and glided forward, his back to the wall. For about sixty feet the going was slow, the tunnel as dark as the bottom of a well. Then he came to where the tunnel veered sharply, and beyond the corner was a dim glow, as if the passageway were lit by a small torch.

Daring a quick glance, Nate saw that the walls themselves were glowing. Or, rather, some kind of peculiar growth that coated them. Phosphorescent lichen, was Nate's best guess. Miners reported it from time to time, but he had never seen some for himself. He continued on with slightly more confidence.

The tunnel angled steadily down, into the very bowels of the earth. Nate traveled hundreds of feet, the stench growing worse by the minute. A grunt warned him beast-men were near, and he slowed.

Stepping to the left side of the tunnel, Nate slunk to within arm's length of an opening. From it wafted dank air and the foulest smell yet. It wasn't another fork. It was a subterranean chamber of immense proportions, the walls aglow as if alive—and it was filled with beast-men.

The creatures lay sprawled in slumber, strewn about as if tumbled by a gale, beast-men and beast-women and beast-children intertwined like strands of hay in a haystack. Remarkably few were snoring. Were it not for the rise and fall of their hairy chests, they might be mistaken for dead.

Nate scoured the chamber for Only Hunts Elk but didn't spot him. Crouching, he hurried past the opening and on down the tunnel. Another chamber loomed, smaller than the first. A dripping noise gave him a clue what he would find, a grotto housing an underground spring, water aplenty for a horde of beast-men. He was about to move on when a sound behind him goaded him into darting to a cluster of boulders and ducking down.

None too soon.

Into the grotto shuffled a beast-man. Half-asleep, it scratched itself as it moved to the spring and knelt to drink. Suddenly it stiffened and sat up, its wide nose dilating. Sniffing repeatedly, the creature rose and glanced uncertainly about.

Nate drew his tomahawk. If the other beast-men were alerted to his presence, he'd never make it out of the cave alive.

The brute came toward the boulders, its beetling brow knit.

Girding himself, Nate leaped, the tomahawk sweeping down. The element of surprise was in his favor, yet even so, the ungodly fast reflexes of the beast-man almost thwarted him. It brought its arm up to ward off the blow, and had Nate not thrown all his weight and strength into the swing, it would have succeeded.

Cold steel severed flesh and sheared through bone to sink into the creature's temple. The beast-man tried to pull back. It opened its mouth, but the sound it wanted to voice died in its throat as its hairy legs buckled and it oozed to the floor like so much melted wax.

Nate tugged the tomahawk free. Leaning the Hawken against a boulder, he took the precaution of dragging the body into the shadows. Then he hurried out.

The tunnel wound deeper into the earth. How deep, it was impossible for Nate to say. He realized that he could search forever and never locate Only Hunts Elk. Common sense dictated he get out of there. But the warrior was his friend, and any man worthy of the name never deserted a friend in need.

Nate hastened on. Around a corner was another chamber, considerably smaller than the others and strewn with stones. He dismissed it as of no consequence and took a step, only to halt when someone groaned.

A vague shape lay against the rear wall. Going over, Nate hunkered next to the object of his quest. Only Hunts

Elk had been bound with strips torn from his own buck-skin shirt.

Palming the Bowie, Nate cut the Shoshone loose, then sheathed the blade and gave the warrior a shake.

Only Hunts Elk groaned again, louder than before.

"Only Hunts Elk!" Nate whispered, shaking harder. "Can you hear me? It is Grizzly Killer."

The man's eyes snapped wide and he started to sit up. "Grizzly—!" he blurted, the rest smothered by Nate's hand.

"Keep quiet! Beast-men are near! We are in their cave!" Nate lowered his palm. "Are you badly hurt? Can you walk without help?"

"Yes, I can walk," Only Hunts Elk said. "My head hurts where one of them hit me with a club, but otherwise I was not harmed."

Nate hoisted the warrior upright. "Use this if you have to," he whispered, giving the Shoshone his tomahawk.

"What about my father and brother?"

"Teeth Like A Beaver is missing. Man Without A Wife and Rabbit Tail are waiting for us outside."

"My son is here in the canyon?" Only Hunts Elk was aghast. "You should not have let him come."

"There was no stopping him," Nate whispered, moving to the passage. He heard nothing to indicate the beast-men were aware their sanctuary had been invaded. Beckoning, he headed for the surface and had gone twenty feet before it dawned on him that the warrior wasn't following.

Only Hunts Elk was leaning against the wall, a hand pressed to a gash in his temple. "I am sorry," he apologized when Nate came back. "I am dizzy. Go on without me and I will catch up."

"Like hell," Nate said in English. Looping an arm around the Shoshone's waist, he started out again. Only Hunts Elk slowly gained strength but still had to be supported when they came to the spring. Stepping to the pool,

Nate lowered him. "Drink some. It should help you. I'll stand guard."

The tunnel was empty but Nate couldn't shake a growing feeling that they were running out of time. Curling his thumb around the Hawken's hammer, he quelled his apprehension.

Only Hunts Elk splashed water on his face, then cupped some and sipped. Rising, he moved with renewed vigor, mustering a grin. "The dizziness is gone. I think I can manage on my own."

All went well until they were half a dozen yards from the chamber in which the beast-men slept. Nate didn't notice movement low down to the floor, and he almost stumbled over a short figure in his path.

It was a child, a beast-boy roughly eight to ten years of age. Sleepily rubbing its eyes, the boy yawned, then saw Nate and Only Hunts Elk. Confusion gave way to comprehension. Throwing back its hairy head, it did what children everywhere did when they were scared. It screamed.

A thrust of the Bowie would have stifled the outcry but Nate couldn't bring himself to slay a child, even a beast-child. "Run!" he directed, and hurtled past the huge chamber.

Wild yowls pealed, inhuman screeches from inhuman lips, and from the chamber bounded stooped shapes, surrounding the child.

"How many are there?" Only Hunts Elk marveled, looking back.

"Trust me, you do not want to know," Nate answered.

Then they had breath only for running, for flying along the tunnel as if endowed with the wings of Mercury. A loud babel of grunts heralded a chorus of outraged shrieks and roars. The beast-men were after them.

Nate wished he had a keg of black powder. One keg was all it would take to blow the cave and seal the creatures in.

"They are gaining on us!" Only Hunts Elk warned.

It sure sounded as if they were. The racket the brutes were making was horrendous, Nate shut it out and devoted his entire will and energy on reaching the entrance. He knew he was close when he flew past the last of the phosphorescent lichen. Speeding along in the dark, he abruptly burst into the cave mouth and nearly collided with Man Without A Wife and Rabbit Tail, who had not stayed outside as they should have.

Only Hunts Elk emerged heartbeats later.

"Father!" the youth declared, and opened his arms to hug him.

"Run!" Nate bawled. "Run for your lives!"

Of the two routes down the bench, Nate deemed the trail the safest. Descending the cliff would take too long, to say nothing of the danger of having the beast-men drop boulders and rocks on them.

Weaving among the piles of bones, Nate sprinted into the open and onto the end of the bench. A glance confirmed the Shoshones were still with him. "Go ahead of me!" he commanded, since he was best able to cover them.

Only Hunts Elk hesitated. "We will not desert you, Grizzly Killer."

"Go! Go!" Nate bellowed, pushing the warrior so hard, Only Hunts Elk nearly tripped. "I'll be right behind you!"

Whirling, Nate leveled the Hawken as the cave reverberated to an unearthly swell of demonic fury. Hulking figures poured from both tunnels in a steady stream, and a writhing wave of incensed troglodytes washed toward the cave mouth—then halted as if they had slammed into an invisible wall.

Nate didn't know what to make of it. By rights the creatures should spew out across the bench in a frenzy. Instead they were milling and howling and shaking their heavy clubs in frustration. It was a full minute before he was willing to accept the fact they weren't going to give chase.

Inexplicably, the beast-men refused to leave their cave. Why was irrelevant, as far as Nate was concerned. Maybe their eyes were weak from generations spent underground and they couldn't tolerate bright sunlight. Or maybe they really *were* superstitious, and it was taboo for them to go abroad during the day.

Nate didn't care what it was, so long as it bought precious time. Rotating on his left heel, he flew down the trail after the Shoshones. The length of his shadow prompted him to look up, and he was appalled to discover how high the sun had climbed. He'd been in the cave a lot longer than he reckoned.

The warriors had reached the bottom of the bench and turned at bay. Only Hunts Elk was caked with sweat and the gash in his temple was bleeding, but he hefted the tomahawk and called out, "Where are they?" as Nate approached.

Man Without A Wife held his lance angled upward. "We will take as many of them with us as we can."

Winded from his long sprint, Nate stopped and doubled over. "No need," he husked. He related the unforeseen but welcome development.

"We might yet escape!" Rabbit Tail said in wonderment.

"I am not leaving Bear Canyon until I know what has befallen your grandfather," Only Hunts Elk stated.

"Then let's find out," Nate said.

On they ran, along the trail to the stream and along the bank to where they had left the poles and logs. They poled across without mishap, then bent their steps toward the rise. They took turns shouting for Teeth Like A Beaver, but the old warrior didn't answer. Less than two hours of daylight remained when they arrived at the breastwork.

Exhausted from lack of sleep and his exertions, Nate slumped to the ground. He hadn't had a wink of rest in nearly thirty-six hours. Another night without would about do him in.

"The rest of you can go on through to the spring," Only Hunts Elk said.

"And leave you to fend for yourself?" Man Without A Wife said. "What kind of brother do you take me for?"

"We should all go," Nate said. Sooner or later they had to accept the fact their father was gone.

"Not while Teeth Like A Beaver is still alive," Only Hunts Elk replied, "and I know he still is."

"You know he is? Or you *hope* he is?" Nate replied.

Rabbit Tail was staring to the north. "Isn't that grandfather there?" he said, pointing.

Nate looked, and damned if there didn't appear to be someone seated cross-legged near where Teeth Like A Beaver had claimed he buried the remains of Bright Morning. Resorting to the spyglass, Nate paid the young man a compliment. "You have the eyes of an eagle, Rabbit Tail."

Man Without A Wife was as astonished as Nate. "It is truly him? Unharmed?"

"What are we waiting for?" Only Hunts Elk scurried excitably off. His son and brother jubilantly bounded after him.

Nate studied the figure a few moments longer; the white-thatched head was bowed, the gnarled hands draped over wizened knees. A hint of a smile touched the weathered face.

Folding the telescope, Nate put it back in the possibles bag and willed his weary legs to move. The Shoshones had quite a lead but he didn't mind so long as he kept them in view. The deathly stillness of the woods no longer bothered him. In a little while he would be lighting a shuck for home and hearth, and within a month Bear Canyon would be no more than a bitter memory.

Exhilaration brought a bounce to Nate's step. All was well that ended well, as old William S. had phrased it.

But his cheerfulness was short lived. It came crashing down around him when a piercing wail keened on the wind.

Only Hunts Elk had reached Teeth Like A Beaver and was on his knees in front of the old warrior, his arms up-flung to the heavens.

Nate ran the rest of the way. When he got there, they had laid Teeth Like A Beaver onto his back, his arms folded across his spindly chest.

"What killed him?" Rabbit Tail was asking. "I do not see any marks on his body."

"There are none," Man Without A Wife verified. "He gave up his spirit, just as he told us he would do."

"Now he is with Bright Morning, his one true love," Only Hunts Elk said. "May he find the happiness that always eluded him."

Nate glanced to the west. Although sunset was a couple of hours away, the sun was about to dip below the west wall. A terrible premonition seized him and he shifted to the northeast, groping for the spyglass again.

"We must honor father's last request," Only Hunts Elk said. "We must bury him right on this spot."

Man Without A Wife poked at the soil with a toe. "The ground is rocky. It will take a while."

"We have time," Only Hunts Elk said.

Nate adjusted the spyglass and the bench came into focus. Not the cave, though. He was too low to see it.

"I will find branches we can dig with," Rabbit Tail offered.

The sun was sinking frightfully fast. Half of it was below the rampart and soon the rest would be. Nate glued the spyglass to the trail down the bench, his hands grown clammy.

"Rocks will do," Only Hunts Elk said, stooping and retrieving one. Jabbing it into the earth, he dislodged a handful of dirt. "We should be done before nightfall."

"We do not have that long," Nate said.

"Why not?" Only Hunts Elk asked.

The sun slipped below the west rim. To the east, a collective horrendous howl resounded and hairy figures spilled over the bench in wave after bloodthirsty wave.

"That's why," Nate said.

Hell had been unbound.

Chapter Twelve

The three Shoshones rose and looked toward the rise. Even without a telescope they could see the bestial horde flowing into the forest.

"Look at them all!" Rabbit Tail blurted in dismay.

"I had no idea there were so many," Man Without A Wife said. "If they find us—"

" 'If'?" Nate broke in. "You mean *when* they find us. Because they will, eventually, unless we slip out through the cleft while we still can. And block it up," he added planning to keep the beast-men from being unleashed on an unsuspecting world.

Only Hunts Elk squatted and resumed digging. "I am burying my father first."

"Cover him with rocks and brush," Nate suggested. It would take much less time. He estimated they only had an hour, maybe less, before the beast-men showed up in their neck of the woods. Some were bound to head for the rise, and if the ogres reached it first, escape would be cut off.

"And have my father eaten by scavengers?" Only Hunts Elk said. "If it were yours, would you dishonor him so?"

But he won't mind, he's dead! Nate wanted to shout. As dead as they would be if they didn't fan the wind. He settled for saying, "It is no longer a matter of what we *want* to do. It is a matter of what we *must* do to stay alive."

"Go if you like," Only Hunts Elk said without looking up, his rock gouging into the soil again and again.

"Can't you reason with him?" Nate asked Man Without A Wife.

The Shoshone glanced to the east, then knelt and clawed at the earth with his bare fingers. "Teeth Like A Beaver was my father, as well."

Rabbit Tail gnawed on his lower lip "I do not want to die. But I will do what I must." Scooping up a stone, he chipped at the ground in a frenetic flurry.

"Hell," Nate said, fixing the spyglass on the bench. It was bare of beast-men by now. Screened by the heavy canopy, the creatures were sweeping toward the stream. They had fallen quiet, as would any predator on the prowl, and Nate couldn't locate them. "Wouldn't you know it?" he said, jerking the spyglass down. Shoving it into his possibles bag, he filled each hand with jagged rocks and tore into the earth as if his life depended on it. Which it did.

"You need not do this," Only Hunts Elk said.

"And buffalo can fly," Nate said.

Dirt and stones and clods flew thick and fast as they scooped and scraped and dug. Soon they had a hole four inches deep, then six, then ten. It was good enough for Nate but the Shoshones kept digging so he persevered, glancing frequently toward the stream so he would know when the beast-men crossed it. Ominously enough, they didn't reappear—as they should have—which added to his foreboding.

The hole was a foot down when Nate straightened. "How deep do you intend to go?" he asked.

"Deep enough so no animal will dig him up," Only Hunts Elk answered.

"You are gambling your life that the beast-men do not find us," Nate mentioned. "One of us should stand watch, at least."

"You do it, Grizzly Killer," Only Hunts Elk said. "You have the glass that sees close."

Nate had no objections. "Hurry," he said, pushing to his feet. "If you love life, hurry." Pivoting, he jogged eastward several dozen yards, to where he could see a long stretch of the stream. The beast-men were still nowhere to be seen.

"Where in tarnation are they?" Nate said aloud.

As if on cue, to the south loping shapes materialized, eight or nine of the throwbacks spread out like wolves on a hunt. But what startled Nate the most was the discovery they were on the *west side of the stream!* Somehow they had crossed without being spotted. And if those few had done it, so had many more.

Nate scanned the trees bordering the waterway, hoping he was wrong but finding otherwise. The forest teemed with brutes. Roaming the spyglass along the shore, he saw a beastly head pop out of the water and a creature heave onto land. It had swum from bank to bank *underwater.*

It was bad. It was very bad. Soon the beast-men would be everywhere. There would be no eluding them. Nate sped to the warriors and relayed the news.

"We are almost done," Only Hunts Elk said.

The grave was now a foot and a half deep.

"Bury him," Nate said. "Bury him *now,* or you might as well dig a hole for your son and your brother. And slit your own throat while you are at it."

The stocky warrior stopped digging. "They are that close?"

"Closer."

Nate was fit to leap for joy when Only Hunts Elk and Man Without A Wife gently lowered Teeth Like A Beaver in. Only Hunts Elk laid the old man's arms at his sides. "I will miss him."

"You will be *joining* him if you do not get this over with," Nate reiterated.

Rabbit Tail had taken an arrow from his quiver and was nocking it to his sinew bow string. He was unusually calm in light of the circumstances. "It is a good day to die," he said.

The two brothers began covering their father. When they didn't move fast enough to suit him, Nate bent and scooped madly at the loose dirt, not caring if they were offended. Gradually, the body disappeared.

"Now all we need do is cover him with branches," Only Hunts Elk said.

Nate resisted an urge to grab the warrior and shake him until his teeth rattled. "We have done enough. Leave him as he is. The beast-men will be here any moment."

"They already are," Rabbit Tail said.

A shadowy silhouette was framed under a tree seventy yards to the northeast. The bone club in its brawny right hand left no doubt as to what it was.

"The thing has seen us," Man Without A Wife said.

"Will it attack or alert the others?" Only Hunts Elk asked no one in particular.

The beast-man did both. Its howls ringing off the cliff, the creature charged in long bound that ate the distance swiftly.

Nate raised the Hawken, but Rabbit Tail took the initiative and sent two glittering shafts into the wildman's torso. The first arrow slowed it, the second brought it to a lurching halt. Snarling ferociously, the beast-man tore at the wooden shafts while tottering another five or six

157

strides, then it pitched over, the body convulsing violently.

"We must reach the cleft," Nate said. Whirling, he raced for his life. Whether the Shoshones mimicked his example was up to them. He had done all he could. Now his top priority was surviving so he could see his wife and daughter again.

Rabbit Tail overtook him. "The others are coming."

Nate glanced over a shoulder. Only Hunts Elk was being pulled along by Man Without A Wife. Abruptly, the older brother stopped dragging his heels and ran for all he was worth.

Howls and roars had broken out all over the place. Beast-men were converging from far and wide.

"We will never make it," Man Without A Wife said.

"Never say never." Nate vaulted a log. Off through the trees black-haired devils flitted toward them like ethereal specters.

"What will we do if they cut us off?" Only Hunts Elk inquired.

Nate grit his teeth in anger. *Why hadn't the warrior thought of that sooner?* "We will fight our way through."

"Against more of them than there are leaves on the trees?" Rabbit Tail exaggerated.

"The more there are, the more we will kill," Nate responded to bolster the youth's courage. Truth told, he could use a little bolstering himself. The odds were hopeless. But so long as a spark of life remained, he wouldn't give up. When he went down, he would go down swinging.

In grim silence they raced on, the thud of their moccasins and their heavy breathing the only sounds. The beast-men were momentarily quiet. Too quiet, Nate felt, a prelude to much worse to come.

The rise was about four hundred yards off. Four hundred yards of dense forest choked with heavy undergrowth. Four hundred yards with beast-men after them every foot of the way.

Nate tried not to dwell on the distance. Pacing himself, he constantly scanned the woods. Furtive forms were loping to intercept them, but so far none were close enough to pose a threat.

An impenetrable thorny thicket barred their way. Nate bore to the right to skirt it and was halfway around when he stumbled on a godsend; a five-foot-deep gully. From where it flanked the thicket, it slanted in the general direction of the rise.

Nate jumped down, ducked low, and jogged on. He had gone some ninety feet when a howl pierced the air and was answered by others. Not howls of rage, but of confusion. The beast-men had lost sight of them and were signaling back and forth.

The gully curved slightly to the left. Nate started to go around the bend, then halted so quickly, Rabbit Tail collided with him. Motioning, Nate dropped low, and the Shoshones followed suit.

Ahead, a beast-man stood at the edge of the gully, its hairy back toward them, scouring the terrain to the south.

Nate gestured for the warriors to back out of sight, which they quietly did. He was almost beyond the bend himself when the beast-man turned. For an instant he thought he had been spotted, but the creature was gazing off up the canyon, and a moment later it trotted into the trees.

"It is gone," Nate whispered.

A straight stretch of gully brought them near the west wall. Flattening, Nate crawled to the top for a look-see. They were now only about two hundred yards from the rise. So close, yet so far.

Only Hunts Elk snaked up next to him. "We should run the rest of the way."

The intervening woods seemed empty, but Nate wasn't willing to risk his life that they really were. "And what if

159

we are spotted? Remember, my wife and daughter are on the other side of that passage. The beast-men must not find it."

"Look!" Only Hunts Elk whispered, extending a finger.

A group of beast-men were east of the rise, nosing into every bush and behind every bole. More were off toward the stream.

Nate glanced overhead. Twilight was descending. Before long night would fall, and the monsters that called Bear Canyon home would be on the prowl.

Only Hunts Elk tilted his own head back. "What do you think, Grizzly Killer? Do we wait for dark or try now?"

"Waiting will do us little good," Nate said. "The beast-men can see at night better than we can. And their sense of smell rivals a dog's. We might as well go now, when we still have some light to see by."

Only Hunts Elk beckoned the others, who crabbed up the incline.

"Keep low," Nate whispered. "If we become separated, get to the rise." He paused. "And if something happens to me, see that Winona and Blue Flower get safely back to our log lodge."

"We will watch over them as if they were our own family," Man Without A Wife promised.

Sliding the Hawken in front of him and holding it with both hands, Nate crawled into a tract of spindly weeds. Advancing, he crawled a few more yards, then stopped to listen.

And on it went until moss-draped trees reared above them. Rising into a crouch, Nate sidled to the nearest.

The beast-men east of the rise were gone. Farther south, Nate reckoned. Easing past the trunk, he padded to the next tree, then to the one after that, always low to the ground, always placing each foot down with care so as not to step on fallen twigs and branches.

The twilight deepened. Across the canyon a rumbling

roar announced a nocturnal nightmare had roused from its den.

Nate dashed to a twisted trunk and leaned against it. To the right the vegetation crackled, and he elevated the Hawken. But it wasn't a beast-man that stepped into the open. It was a small animal, its head and body reminiscent of a full-grown horse; yet it stood barely three feet high. Rating it no threat, Nate let the muzzle drop.

The tiny horse saw him. It stepped back in fright, then let out with a high-pitched whinny, a whinny loud enough to be heard clear down by the stream.

Nate took a step, waving an arm to shoo the little horse off, but the damage had been done. Feral howls burst from undergrowth to the southeast, and out of the brush lumbered a trio of beast-men.

"They have found us!" Nate cried, and broke for the rise as the woods were rocked by a well-nigh deafening discord. The three beast-men moved to cut him off but he didn't shoot. Not yet, not until they were so close he couldn't possibly miss.

"There are more behind us!" Only Hunts Elk hollered.

And more to the east, Nate saw. He ran full out, the Shoshones hard on his heels.

"We will never make it!" Man Without A Wife declared.

The three beast-men were closing rapidly. Hefting their heavy clubs, they shrieked like demented Comanches.

Another ten yards, and Nate stopped and brought the Hawken to bear. As the foremost brute filled the sights, he stroked the trigger. The rifle belched smoke and lead, impaling the beast-man in midstride. Tumbling wildly, the body came to rest in a disjointed pile.

The others never broke stride.

Nate yanked out a pistol and took aim. He was able to save the lead, though, because an arrow had transfixed the second brute's chest and the creature sprawled onto its belly. That left the third beast-man, but a lance met it head-on.

"Keep going!" Only Hunts Elk cried.

Nate didn't need prompting. With a savage din ringing in his ears, he covered the final hundred yards and came to the bottom of the rise. Spinning, he counted nine on-rushing beast-men, with more back among the trees. "Keep going! I will cover you!"

None of the Shoshones listened. They took stands on either side of him, Man Without A Wife drawing his knife. Rabbit Tail had an arrow nocked, and another in his mouth ready to be used next.

"It has been an honor knowing you, Grizzly Killer," Only Hunts Elk shouted to be heard above the baying of the two-legged pack.

"We are not dead yet," Nate responded, his fingers a blur as he attempted to reload the Hawken before the beast-men reached them.

Only Hunts Elk looked at his son. "I suppose it would be useless for me to ask you to go."

The youth snatched the arrow from his mouth to declare, "Just as you would not desert your father, I will not leave you."

Only Hunts Elk gripped Rabbit Tail's arm. "You have always been a dutiful son. Do not disappoint me now."

The issue was decided for them. A screeching beast-man hurtled at Only Hunts Elk and was stopped cold by an arrow to the ribs. Snarling, the creature lunged, but Rabbit Tail sent a second shaft into it.

"I love you, father," the young man said.

"And I love you."

Then there was no time for talk, no time for anything other than fighting for their lives. Half a dozen beast-men were upon them, clubs swinging, growls and roars mixed in fiendish refrain.

Nate jerked up the Hawken and fired at point-blank range into the belly of an oncoming brute. Ducking under a vicious blow, he skipped backward and yanked out a pistol, firing just as the beast-man raised the club to try again.

Another wildman was about to cave in Man Without A Wife's skull. Quickly switching the spent pistol to the same hand that held the Hawken, Nate drew his second flintlock and fired a fraction of an instant before the fatal blow could descend.

All six ogres were down but so was Only Hunts Elk, a wicked wound in his left shoulder. Rabbit Tail slid an arm around his father and boosted him erect.

"Up the rise!" Nate shouted. Shoving both pistols under his belt, he commenced to reload the rifle while retreating toward the top.

Man Without A Wife came last. He had helped himself to a bone club and gave it a few swings, getting the feel of the weapon.

Blood was oozing from Only Hunts Elk's raptured flesh. Grimacing, he said, "I can manage on my own. Go ahead of me. I will only slow you down."

"Save your breath for fighting," Man Without A Wife said.

On all sides, beast-men were flowing from the forest. But instead of surging up the slope, they gathered around the bodies of their companions, a few of whom were still alive.

Nate was shocked when one of the newcomers struck a severely stricken beast-man across the throat, dispatching him. Seconds later another blood-soaked abomination was put out of its misery.

"Look at them," Only Hunts Elk said in disgust. "Not even animals are so cruel,"

More creatures were arriving every few seconds. Before long there would be a veritable legion, more than enough to overwhelm three men and a stripling.

Nate gained the crest and passed through the opening the bear had made. In the last few minutes the sky had drastically darkened. When the final attack came, they wouldn't be able to see the beast-men until the creatures were right on top of them. "We need a fire."

"I will help gather wood," Man Without A Wife said.

Swiftly, they stacked what they could find in front of the opening. Nate's fire steel and flint ignited a handful of dry grass, and as the flames licked skyward, the darkness was broken by guttural grunts from below.

"What are they waiting for?" Rabbit Tail anxiously asked.

"Be grateful they delay at all," Only Hunts Elk said. He had sunk onto a log and was staunching the flow of blood with his fingers.

"Their next attack will be the last," Man Without A Wife remarked.

No one had to ask what he meant.

Glancing at Nate, Only Hunts Elk said, "Have you thought of a way to block the cleft so the animal-men can not get through?"

"Not yet." Nate faced the opening, barely discernible in the gloom. "But there has to be a way." He grasped his powder horn so he could reload a pistol, then gave a start.

"What is it?" Only Hunts Elk inquired.

"An idea," Nate replied. The horn was two-thirds full; it contained enough black powder to produce a powerful explosion if the powder were set off all at once. A blast sufficient, perhaps, to seal the cleft for all eternity. The key would be to place it at the proper spot.

The beast-men began howling and yipping and roaring, working themselves into a killing frenzy.

Nate grabbed a brand from the fire. "I need to check something. If I am right, all of us will greet the dawn."

"Do what you must," Only Hunts Elk said. "We will keep them from the passage."

Nate streaked into the cleft and on down the narrow defile, scraping his shoulder and an elbow in his reckless haste. Thirty feet in, as he recalled, the walls narrowed to their narrowest point. Reaching it, he held the brand aloft. Hairline cracks laced the arched ceiling like so many spider webs.

"It just might work!" Nate said out loud. Kneeling, he dug at the base of the left wall, and when he had a hole big enough for the powder horn, he placed the horn in it. Drawing his knife, he hurriedly cut a twelve-inch strip from his buckskin shirt. Then, opening the horn, he wadded the end of the strip into the horn to serve as a fuse.

Now all he had to do was get the Shoshones and go! Grinning, Nate ran back down the passage. He was almost to the end when colossal roars and clarion war whoops broke out. Another stride brought him out onto the bench and into chaos run riot.

The beast-men were swarming up over the rise in an unending wave. But the breastwork had slowed those in front, creating a tangle of hairy bodies. Some were trying to swarm in through the broken section but were being deterred by the fire. Veering aside, they added to the confusion.

Only Hunts Elk and Man Without A Wife were up on the barrier, resisting to their utmost. Man Without A Wife was striking right and left with the bone club. Only Hunts Elk was hacking at beastly heads and shoulders with Nate's tomahawk.

Behind them. Rabbit Tail was employing his bow to terrible effect.

"Into the passage!" Nate shouted, but they couldn't hear him above the tumult. Casting the brand down, he aimed the Hawken at a beast-man about to climb over the top. At his shot, the creature catapulted down onto its fellows.

"Into the passage!" Nate repeated, rushing to lend a hand. Pulling his Bowie, he leaped onto the breastwork and hacked at the rising hairy tide in a frenzy born of raw desperation. Five, six, seven beast-men fell trying to get at him.

To Nate's left a furious struggle had ensued. Shifting, he was dismayed to see Man Without A Wife down, flat on the dank earth with a crude spear protruding from the center of his chest. Several beast-man had gained the upper log and were raining blows on Only Hunts Elk, who was weakly warding them off and would not last much longer.

Nate moved toward him but was confronted by a pair of snarling visages.

Rabbit Tail stepped in close, his bow twanging. One of the beast-men trying to kill his father dropped. The string twanged again, and a third time, clearing space for his father to jump down. But just as Only Hunts Elk turned, a wooden club descended with the force of a thunderclap and crushed the rear of his cranium to splinters.

"Father!" Lowering his bow, forgetting his own safety, Rabbit Tail dashed to Only Hunts Elk and bent over him.

Nate's Bowie sheared into a hairy jugular. Suddenly in the clear, he leaped toward the Shoshones and was in midair when a heavy lance flashed out of the night and impaled the youth from shoulder blade to stomach.

Rabbit Tail never looked up, never uttered a sound. Collapsing onto Only Hunts Elk, he twitched once and was still.

Nate was beside himself. Grabbing the bone club next to Man Without A Wife, he spun, at bay. He swung once, twice, three times, and with each swing a beast-man fell. But he was only delaying the inevitable. A living wall of murderous brutes were scrambling over the breastwork. At any moment he would be inundated in a flood of muscle and hair.

Whirling, Nate ran to the fire and snagged another brand. A charging beast-man tried to bring him down but Nate flung the bone club into's its contorted face. Pivoting, he sprinted for the cleft and reached it mere steps ahead of a knot of enraged pursuers.

Plunging into the passage, Nate sped to the powder

horn. As he leaned down, he glanced back.

The creatures were milling at the entrance. In another few moments they would enter.

Nate touched the brand to the fuse. Sputtering, the buckskin caught and burned—much more rapidly than he had counted on. Thrusting the torch ahead of him, he fled for his life with roars reverberating off the narrow walls.

Every second was an eternity of suspense. Nate didn't know how long he had. It could be sixty seconds or it could be six. He sped past a bend. Past another. Up ahead, the other end of the cleft appeared, and just when he thought he would make it, the powder exploded.

For a moment nothing happened. Then, from overhead, came a gigantic grinding noise, and the walls and ceiling seemed to shake and sway.

Nate launched himself at the opening as a blast of air and dust swirled about him. There was a mammoth rending and booming crash. He was barely aware of sailing out into the night, of landing on his side and rolling over and over.

The torch was lying in the dirt but it still burned. Grabbing it, Nate rose and marveled at his own handiwork. The cleft had closed! Not entirely, but the only way the beast-men would ever get out of Bear Canyon was if they shrank to the size of badgers. The land of legend was forever cut off from the rest of the world.

Slowly, wearily, Nate King turned toward the spring. Toward his wife and daughter and a future where the only howls that wavered on the wind would be those of wolves and coyotes.

As it was meant to be.

Jane Candia Coleman

THE O'KEEFE EMPIRE

Alex O'Keefe has a dream. Fired up with visions of an empire and millions of acres for the taking in New Mexico Territory, he sets out from Texas to make his dream a reality. His wife, Joanna, becomes caught up in her husband's enthusiasm, sells the family holdings, then boards a train to meet him. She has no idea what lies before her. When Joanna arrives, her own dreams are nearly shattered. Alex is dead, murdered by an unknown killer. And the empire they had planned is threatened by exorbitant cattle fees charged by the railroad. But dreams die hard. Joanna will do whatever she has to, even if that means taking the cattle on a brutal overland trail drive to San Diego, across the Mojave Desert.

___4859-0 $4.50 US/$5.50 CAN

Gary McCarthy

THE BUFFALO HUNTERS

Thomas Atherton is a young stable master from Massachusetts who has always dreamed of leaving Boston behind and heading west across the great frontier. When he meets the legendary Buffalo Bill Cody at his famous Wild West Show, Thomas decides the time has finally come to make his dream a reality. He sees his chance when he hears about a $5,000 reward offered to the first man to find a surviving herd of the nearly extinct buffalo. And so he sets out to test his mettle on a buffalo hunt. But he will soon find that taming horses is nothing compared with taming the prairie and the rugged mountains beyond—or surviving runins with vicious outlaws and rustlers.

___4884-1 $3.99 US/$4.99 CAN

WILDERNESS
Savages

David Thompson

Frontiersmen living in the untamed Rockies are surrounded every day by endless dangers, including attack by hostile Indians. But to Nate King and his family, the local tribes are simply people like them, people trying to live free in the glorious mountains, and many of them have become their friends. It is only when Nate's son, Zach, sets out with his fiancée to visit her relatives in St. Louis that Zach meets savages of a very different kind—vicious white cutthroats who kidnap his beloved. Zach is far from home, with much to learn if he hopes to save the woman he loves. But he knows one thing—he'll save her if it's the last thing he does. Then he'll give those savages a dose of civilizing . . . frontier style.

___4711-X $3.99 US/$4.99 CAN

THE BLOODY QUARTER

LES SAVAGE, JR.

Paul Hagar has always had hard luck. He's drifted through the Southwest, trying his hand at a few different things, but always with no success. Then it looks like his luck has changed. He has a chance to file for land in the most important quarter section in all of Converse County, Wyoming. Known as the Bloody Quarter, the strip serves as a gateway for the surrounding ranchers to summer graze their herds in the high country. But it is called the Bloody Quarter for a reason—some pretty ruthless ranchers are willing to do just about anything to control it. Even commit murder. Paul Hagar's luck might have changed, all right . . . but for the worse.

___4863-9 $4.50 US/$5.50 CAN

Dorchester Publishing Co., Inc.
P.O. Box 6640
Wayne, PA 19087-8640

Please add $2.50 for shipping and handling for the first book and $.75 for each book thereafter. NY, NYC, and PA residents, please add appropriate sales tax. No cash, stamps, or C.O.D.s. All orders shipped within 6 weeks via postal service book rate. Canadian orders require $2.50 extra postage and must be paid in U.S. dollars through a U.S. banking facility.

Name_____
Address_____
City_____State_____Zip_____
I have enclosed $_____ in payment for the checked book(s).
Payment <u>must</u> accompany all orders. ❑ Please send a free catalog.
      CHECK OUT OUR WEBSITE! www.dorchesterpub.com

. . . and coming
May 2001
from. . .

LEISURE
BOOKS

Man From Wolf River

John D. Nesbitt

Owen Felver is just passing through. He is on his way from the Wolf River down to the Laramie Mountains for some summer wages. He makes his camp outside of Cameron, Wyoming, and rides in for a quick beer. But it isn't quick enough. While he is there he sees pretty, young Jenny—and the puffed-up gent trying to get rude with her. What else can he do but step in and defend her? Right after that some pretty tough thugs start to make it clear Felver isn't all too welcome around town. Trouble is, the more they tell him to move on—and the more he sees of Jenny—the more he wants to stay. He knows they have something to hide, but he has no idea just how awful it is—or how far they will go to keep it hidden.

___4871-X $4.50 US/$5.50 CAN

Dorchester Publishing Co., Inc.
P.O. Box 6640
Wayne, PA 19087-8640

Please add $2.50 for shipping and handling for the first book and $.75 for each book thereafter. NY, NYC, and PA residents, please add appropriate sales tax. No cash, stamps, or C.O.D.s. All orders shipped within 6 weeks via postal service book rate. Canadian orders require $2.50 extra postage and must be paid in U.S. dollars through a U.S. banking facility.

Name_____
Address_____
City_____ State_____ Zip_____
I have enclosed $_____ in payment for the checked book(s).
Payment **must** accompany all orders. ❑ Please send a free catalog.
    CHECK OUT OUR WEBSITE! www.dorchesterpub.com

LAURAN PAINE

THE KILLER GUN

It is no ordinary gun. It is specially designed to help its owner kill a man. George Mars has customized a Colt revolver so it will fire when it is on half cock, saving the time it takes to pull back the hammer before firing. But then the gun is stolen from Mars's shop. Mars has engraved his name on it but, as the weapon passes from hand to hand, owner to owner, killer to killer, his identity becomes as much of a mystery as why possession of the gun skews the odds in any duel. And the legend of the killer gun grows with each newly slain man.

___4875-2 $4.50 US/$5.50 CAN

Dorchester Publishing Co., Inc.
P.O. Box 6640
Wayne, PA 19087-8640

Please add $2.50 for shipping and handling for the first book and $.75 for each book thereafter. NY, NYC, and PA residents, please add appropriate sales tax. No cash, stamps, or C.O.D.s. All orders shipped within 6 weeks via postal service book rate. Canadian orders require $2.50 extra postage and must be paid in U.S. dollars through a U.S. banking facility.

Name_____
Address_____
City_____State_____Zip_____
I have enclosed $ _____ in payment for the checked book(s).
Payment <u>must</u> accompany all orders. ❑ Please send a free catalog.
CHECK OUT OUR WEBSITE! www.dorchesterpub.com

MEN BEYOND THE LAW

These three short novels showcase Max Brand doing what he does best: exploring the wild, often dangerous life beyond the constraints of cities, beyond the reach of civilization . . . beyond the law. Whether he's a desperate man fleeing the tragic results of a gunfight, an innocent young man who stumbles onto the loot from a bank robbery, or the gentle giant named Bull Hunter—one of Brand's most famous characters—each protagonist is out on his own, facing two unknown frontiers: the Wild West . . . and his own future.

___4873-6 $4.50 US/$5.50 CAN